'Another splendidly surreal book ~~from~~ ~~~~ ~~~~ ~~~~
Beautifully written, with a splendid eye for the inconsequential
detail'   Jennifer Paterson, *Spectator*

'The late flowering of Andrew Barrow as a comic genius has
been one of the most refreshing events of modern fiction . . .
Full of insight into our failure to connect, the book is sad,
funny, even haunting'   Hugh Massingberd, *Oldie*

'Barrow does not just observe – where the bias is visual –
he also successfully captures registers of speech . . .
A single word, looking no more than utilitarian, often
evokes a whole personality'
Hal Jensen, *Times Literary Supplement*.

'The worlds we look at are terrifyingly real: one feels, not as if
one were reading a novel, but as if one were somehow
overhearing real conversation through thin partition walls. At
no point can the reader comfort himself with the thought that
this is, after all, only fiction'   David McLaurin, *Catholic Herald*

'Wonderful precision . . . the strangely impressive small talk
which he records is the very opposite of professional jokes'
Penelope Fitzgerald, *Evening Standard*

'*The Man In the Moon* is not only an extraordinary display of
what the huge ears and dissecting blade of Mr Barrow can do
when they are loosed upon the unconnected babble of those
upon whom he eavesdrops, it is also a brilliant, hilarious and
highly disturbing testament to what careless talk reveals . . .
Imagine *The Waste Land* written by Harold Pinter'
Alan Coren, *Spectator*

Andrew Barrow was born in Lancashire in 1945. He is the author of five works of non-fiction, including *Gossip* and *The Great Book of Small Talk*. His acclaimed, prize-winning first novel, *The Tap Dancer*, is published by Picador.

ANDREW BARROW

The Man
In The Moon

PICADOR

First published 1996 by Picador

This edition published 1998 by Picador
an imprint of Macmillan Publishers Ltd
25 Eccleston Place, London SW1W 9NF
and Basingstoke

Associated companies throughout the world

ISBN 0 330 35303 9

1 3 5 7 9 8 6 4 2

A CIP catalogue record for this book is available from
the British Library.

Typeset by SetSystems Ltd, Saffron Walden, Essex
Printed and bound in Great Britain by
Mackays of Chatham plc, Chatham, Kent

January 1965

THE MAN IN THE MOON stood at a busy crossroads about six miles from the city centre. Fast-moving traffic roared and rattled past its windows, which were decorated with posters proclaiming 'Top Line Variety' and 'Star Names Every Night'.

I entered the building, made myself known to the barmaid and was directed to a small room behind the empty bandstand.

Here, a grey-haired man was attending to his make-up in front of a mirror.

'Are you the comedian?' he asked as he zipped himself into a purple suit.

I had obtained the work on the telephone. Within minutes of arriving in the city, I had dialled the number of a theatrical agent whose name was listed on the back page of *The Stage*. A man with a timid, girlish voice asked, 'Have you got an act?' 'Yes,' I lied. 'Hold on a moment,' he said softly. Then after a few seconds' whispering, he had offered me a week's work at The Man In The Moon.

'You don't look like a comedian,' said the man in the purple suit but he was suddenly distracted by the sound of female laughter. 'Our guest star has arrived,' he said proudly.

A buxom blonde soon sailed into the room wearing a pink and white gown and was followed by a dapper young man carrying a sequin-covered jacket on a dry-cleaner's hanger. As I took off my camel-hair coat, I realized I was the only person present with no special costume and no make-up to put on.

'Now, children,' began the man in the purple suit. 'Nine o'clock start, all right?'

Then he turned to me and, eyeing my white face and pin-striped suit, said, 'You all right, William?'

In answer to the questions that followed, I admitted that this was my first appearance in the north of England but let it be known that I had made quite a number of appearances in the south.

'Which rooms have you worked down there, William?' asked the dapper young man.

Soon there were sounds of the saloon bar filling up and flashing coloured lights round the bandstand cast lively reflections backstage. Then the music began, muffled notes and chord changes before the cabaret.

'Okay, let's get in there,' said the buxom blonde.

The show began with our guest star singing 'You're My World' and other new songs in a loud confident voice. The man in the purple suit shouted against the applause that The Lovely Miss Gay Gordon would be back on stage later.

He then announced my act.

I stepped up on to the bandstand and began to relate the material which I had hurriedly assembled after being given the booking .

'I've just come from London by air. It's the only way to fly.'

This first joke got a few titters from the sixty or so people present.

'I slept like a log last night. I woke up in the fireplace,' I continued cautiously. Within half a minute, I had lost the audience's attention. I never regained it. In the corner, someone began playing a fruit machine, while closer to the stage, someone else began telling their own jokes to a friend. At the end of my four minutes, the man in the purple suit jumped to the microphone and ordered, 'A round of applause for William!' I shouted, 'Goodnight, everybody,' blew a kiss at the audience and skipped off the stage to join Miss Gay Gordon and the others at a table marked 'Artistes Only'.

'Great voice,' I told the guest star.

'I pride myself on it,' she replied.

She then complimented me on my act and began to quiz me about my background. 'Come to see how the other half lives?' she asked darkly.

That night thick smog enveloped the centre of the city and I had difficulty finding the hotel where I was staying. It was to be my last night there anyway. The following morning, I moved to a bed-and-breakfast place in the suburbs. In the evening, I returned to The Man In The Moon and forgot my words.

The next day, a letter from the agent was waiting for me at the pub.

'I am sorry to say that The Man In The Moon are not pleased with your work and have asked me to replace you for the rest of the week. Will you kindly then finish there tonight Wednesday.'

July 1966

VIEWED FROM A DISTANCE, the cinema seemed to dominate one side of the Lambeth Road. Posters advertising *The League of Gentlemen*, starring Jack Hawkins, adorned its foyer, which was approached by a peculiar outside staircase and a gallery.

On this gallery, as I made my way towards the building for the first time, a white egg was moving.

I climbed the staircase and found that this pale oval object was the head of a fat old man in red and gold uniform. I was beginning to speak to him when a smaller figure in blue evening dress shot out of a side office.

I recognized this man from a framed photograph on the staircase. 'Your host is Mr Horace Hill' read the caption under a black and white photograph of a worried-looking man with crinkly hair.

In real life, Mr Hill was as rugged and wrinkled as an uprooted tree but he wore a woman's ring on one finger.

'Have you been in cinemas before?' he asked nervously.

Then he said, 'Once you get used to the hours, it's all right.'

The red-uniformed commissionaire, whose name was Arthur, began rattling utensils in the passage and presently showed his large pale face in the office.

'D' you take sugar in tea, William?'

Then Mr Hill asked, 'What time will you have your lunch, William?'

I had been recruited as assistant manager but soon found that Mr Hill was too cautious to delegate work to me. Left to my own devices, I wandered into the small auditorium and watched a newsreel about the Queen's visit to a football match, then a trailer featuring Alfred Hitchcock.

'I welcome you all here and feel sure we shall see some fine football,' said the Queen.

'How do you do?' said Alfred Hitchcock. 'I would like to tell you about my latest motion picture *Marnie*.'

Other staff at the cinema consisted of two projectionists, who worked up in the roof, a tough little lady in the kiosk downstairs, who sold sweets and cigarettes as well as tickets, and four part-time usherettes. Mavis Pinter, Ethel Pretty, Myrtle Eastern and Brenda Bacon were their names. The two on duty often chatted in the foyer.

'I'm just fed up with this afternoon.'

'It's warm in here. It's terribly cold outside. I said to Myrtle I wish I'd put a cardigan on.'

'You know who I saw today. Your ex-boyfriend. I'm joking now. You know, the chatterbox.'

Mavis was the longest reigning of the usherettes. Her grey hair was swept up into a coif at the front and tied in a neat black sack at the back. Her companion was a more homely figure: a pink cardigan with large brass buttons protruded from under her uniform.

Arthur knew the schedule.

'Must be getting near sales time, Brenda.'

Brenda later emerged through the heavy red curtains and said, 'Sold five tubs.'

I soon returned to the auditorium and found Jack Hawkins addressing his gang of thieves on the night before the robbery.

'So relax, get a good night's sleep and good luck.'

I took a seat in the back row and remained undisturbed for forty minutes.

'Give them their money's worth at the trial,' said the gang leader's friend at the end of the film. 'Then flog your memoirs to the Sunday papers. There's always an angle.'

Then the Queen was back, followed by Alfred Hitchcock.

'*Marnie* is not *Psycho*. Nor do we have hundreds of birds flapping about pecking people willy-nilly.'

My first day at the cinema ended shortly before midnight, watching Mr Hill count the takings. He flicked through the notes with a sinister smile and then pushed them into a round leather bag.

'After we've cashed up, you can get away if you like.'

He then walked me down the street to place the bag in the night safe of a local bank.

As we trotted along together, I tried to ask Mr Hill about the usherettes.

'Myrtle's a good sort, isn't she?'

Mr Hill made no reply so I rephrased the question. 'Myrtle works hard, doesn't she?'

'She works hard, yes,' said Mr Hill after another pause but his mind remained focused on more fundamental matters. If ever there was any money missing at the end of the day, he explained, he would make it up with his own cash. 'It's costing me a fortune,' he said.

Mr Hill faced a further burden the following morning, when the chief projectionist's wife telephoned to say that her husband had been taken to hospital during the night. For a few hours, Mr Hill was obliged to operate the 'Projectormatic' himself.

While he was occupied in this way, I examined the office carefully.

A number of memos from Head Office were pinned on a notice-board. One was headed, 'Procedure to be followed in the event of the death of a patron'.

There was also a large calendar with various jottings on it. Against one week in August was written, 'Mrs Pretty. Holiday in the sun', to which someone had pencilled a question mark.

Under Mr Hill's desk was a lost property box, containing a Bible in a zip-up case, gloves and purses galore, a boy's cap bearing the label of a school outfitters and a roll of green crêpe paper.

On the top of the desk was a letter from a patron, beginning with the words, 'Why, oh, why, must we have these terrible cartoon films? They are an insult to the intelligence of an adult audience.'

There was also a large pad covered in desperate, urgent-looking doodles.

In the afternoon the assistant projectionist arrived – he wore a prickly red tweed jacket – and Mr Hill was able to leave for a late lunch break.

He returned in an animated state.

'George has just arrived. It's about his time.'

Mr Hill took a bemused interest in a character by this name, who seemed to inhabit the area and often stood outside the cinema shouting abuse.

'Did you see him? He stood here and then there. Come and stand here and you'll hear him in a moment.'

I soon saw a big man like a boxer dog being moved along by two policemen.

'George used to work in the cinema,' Mr Hill explained. 'He sued the manager for assault.'

I nipped back into the auditorium and watched the closing sequence of *The League of Gentlemen*.

'Give them their money's worth at the trial,' I heard for the third or fourth time. 'Then flog your memoirs to the Sunday papers. There's always an angle.'

Outside in the foyer, Mr Hill went on talking about George.

'At Christmas time, he has a truck loaded with toys and books, cheap little books ... Oh yes, they all go, and sometimes he sells bottles of spirits, whisky and gin, on the cheap ... No, I've never bought any but you get them quite cheap though, about four shillings cheaper.'

He then retreated to his office and made a long and mysterious call to the manager of another cinema in the same chain. 'Well, that's it,' he said. 'The company'll soon whip the money off me if I'm short. It's a bit risky, isn't it? If you get any more you have to have them kicking around the office floor and that's where the trouble starts.'

While talking, Mr Hill had drawn a picture on his pad of a hydrogen bomb exploding.

During Mr Hill's days off, a relief manager, Mr Diamond, moved in. Taller and sleeker than Mr Hill, he tackled the job in a more aggressive and exuberant manner.

'I'm giving an interval of five minutes at six-thirty,' he announced. Then, on discovering some discrepancy in the stock sheets, 'Oh, dearie me, such is life,' and, after further reflection, 'Cockneys are fiddlers.'

Later in the day, he said, 'You must be bored,' and then added, 'I sometimes wonder if there is such a thing as an interesting job.'

A kind-hearted man, he was soon wrapping up two copies of *Cine Weekly* to send to the sick projectionist – slipping in two pound notes and remarking as he did so, 'There's no money in hospital.'

The next day, two figures from Head Office called on a regular inspection tour.

'We had the usual chitchat,' Mr Diamond said afterwards. Then he confided, 'They rush their managers and assistant managers around like cattle. They may well decide they don't want us two.'

The following morning, he confessed, 'This is the queerest damn set-up I've ever run into.'

'Did you have a nice two days?' I asked Mr Hill on his return.

'Yes, quite nice, thank you. Quite nice indeed.'

Mr Hill did not talk about his time off any further. He appeared neither to enjoy his work nor his leisure. His only indulgences were his long lunch hours, which he used to get right out of the area.

'The trip over to Leicester Square makes a bit of an

outing. It's a long day. I was on the train at eight-twenty this morning. Sunbury.'

He often told me what he had for lunch.

'I had steak pudding,' he might say. 'Once you got through the suet 'twasn't bad.'

One afternoon I found Mr Hill dabbing at his blue dinner suit with a sponge. 'It's all right, thanks,' he said. 'Just a few grease spots. I had fried chicken for lunch and splashed myself a bit.'

Then he told me excitedly that his friend George had been arrested for begging and sentenced to a month's imprisonment.

That afternoon, the audience was unsettled. Children chattered their way through an Abbott and Costello movie – and I heard a patron snapping open and shut a suitcase. There was a rustling of crisp packets and a gurgle of pop bottles being sucked empty of their last drops.

I emerged to hear one of the usherettes protesting, 'I'm not coming in – I'm not taking it any more. You're not 'appy with people like that.'

I found Arthur resting halfway down the stairs. Then he moved and stood out on the pavement, a solid but solitary figure. He explained, 'I shall be at it tonight. Half-past eight to half-past nine. Changing publicity.'

Later that day, posters advertising *The League of Gentlemen* were replaced by ones advertising Alfred Hitchcock's *Marnie*.

I had been at the cinema for at least two weeks before I climbed the narrow staircase to the projection room. Here I found metal drums labelled 'Inflammable Film. Worthless

If Damaged' and the junior projectionist reading a showbiz magazine. He wore his usual tweed jacket. From inside the machinery came the cheery sound of a 'Loony' cartoon, then that of violent violins.

'What's that?' I asked.

'Start of the big feature,' he replied.

Mr Hill began to entrust me with a few duties. I assisted with the stocktaking – 'Tip the ice lollies out and count them. Tip them out and count them' – and was occasionally required to seat the patrons. These came in dribs and drabs. A soldier carried two bars of Nestlé's milk chocolate bought at the kiosk. A hairless youth asked me about the new Elvis Presley film. One patron's breath smelt. Another called me 'Sir' .

I also had to direct people to the toilets. These were inconveniently placed on the ground floor.

'They've used the back stairs before now,' complained Mr Hill.

Among the stream of customers one day came one of the men from Head Office. Although it was hot – now the middle of the summer – he wore an overcoat and silk scarf. For a fraction of a second, he tried to balance his briefcase on the brass rail at the top of the staircase.

He wanted to know the whereabouts of Arthur, the commissionaire.

'He's gone on his break,' said Mr Hill.

The man from Head Office said he was going on holiday himself soon.

'Going anywhere nice?' enquired Mr Hill.

After the man had left, Mr Hill asked me, 'Do you

still not want to be a manager?' and then, more sharply, 'Why, what's wrong with it?'

'Nothing at all,' I replied.

'Help me! Oh, God, somebody help me!' the heroine of Alfred Hitchcock's *Marnie* was screaming next time I entered the auditorium. I stayed till the end of the programme and the National Anthem, for which no one ever stood up. When the house lights went on I found the floor was covered with sweet wrappers, disused cartons and empty pop bottles – several large bags could be filled with this mess. One patron was still asleep and needed waking up. Another was wandering around the gallery outside.

'Oh, look,' I said. 'Look, there's an old man hanging about. Is all well?'

Mr Hill immediately left his desk and said to the intruder, 'Can I help you? This is the way out. You went the wrong way.'

'He's been coming here for years,' he said later and I would not let the subject alone.

'Do you know his name?' I asked.

'No, not a clue,' said Mr Hill as he began to cash up.

Mr Hill prepared for his days off carefully, leaving a note for Mr Diamond saying, 'Please give these chocolates to Mrs Windmill morning cleaner. Will give you a ring. Horace.' In the event, Mr Diamond was out when Mr Hill telephoned and the lady in the kiosk took the call. 'I've just had Mr Hill on the line,' she said proudly. 'He said, "What sort of day have we had, Lucy?"'

A few days later, Mr Hill poured out his troubles. He had

only come to London under pressure from his wife. Until four years ago he had been managing a cinema in a remote town in East Anglia but his wife was bored with provincial life. His main complaint about his current existence was the lack of social life.

'Monday and Tuesday I have off but then all my friends are at work . . .'

He hankered for the time before he had entered cinema management when he and his wife had run a guest house in Frinton.

One afternoon when Mr Hill was downstairs managing the kiosk, I opened the drawer of his desk. Inside I found a paper bag containing two slices of ham and a small square lump of cheese. Beside it was a tiny tin of boned chicken. There was also an account book with entries for 'rent', 'coal' and 'telephone'. Then I came upon a silver cigarette case inscribed 'for H from J. July 5, 1945'.

Suddenly, a delivery man with a piece of paper in his hand swung his head through the doorway and said, 'Are you going to sign this, chief, or the bloke downstairs?'

Then I wandered back into the cinema where the small afternoon audience was watching the heroine of *Marnie* being cross-examined by Mr Rutland, played by Sean Connery. 'Did you have a tough childhood, Mrs Taylor?' 'Not particularly.' 'I think you did. I think you've had a hard tough climb . . .'

Arthur the commissionaire had also known happier times. He told me he had once owned five chip shops in Warrington. He still kept some of the frying equipment at home but his catering activities were now confined to brewing tea for the staff of the cinema.

His life was made more difficult by his bouts of drinking.

One day I heard Arthur and an usherette yelling at each other.

'I'm going home,' said the usherette.

'Listen, Brenda, I said nothing,' shouted Arthur.

In the end, it was Arthur who went home. When he failed to appear the following morning, Mr Hill said calmly, 'He often does this. He'll turn up again in four or five days' time.'

This the old man did, carrying with him a certificate of unfitness to work signed by a doctor in Canonbury. One of his first duties was to change the publicity again. After a ten-day run, *Marnie* was being replaced by the Elvis Presley film, *G.I. Blues*.

The following day, Mr Hill's wife – was she the 'J' of the cigarette case? – called at the cinema. It was hard to see this cosy woman as the architect of her husband's troubles, but later Mr Hill told me, 'We've been separated twice. Last week was only the second time we've been out this year. We've been married twenty-one years.' And I gathered that he had come to London to try and save the relationship.

Meanwhile a certain tender rapport had blossomed between Mr Hill and the stately usherette named Mavis Pinter. One day she came into work with a package for him. It contained the top half of his blue dinner suit, which she had taken home to clean and darn.

Another afternoon, Mr Hill stopped chasing around

with stock sheets and sat down at his desk to write a
letter.

'Dear Mavis,' he began.

Mr Hill's next two days off coincided with the final of the
World Cup. Mr Diamond listened to this excitedly on his
transistor radio.

'By golly, they've equalized! It's going to be some
game!'

When it was over, he braced himself to enter the
cinema and announce the result to the audience.

'Okay, let's get in there,' he said.

Later we sat chatting in the office.

'What are you doing in this business? With your
brains?' he asked suddenly.

I then spoke briefly about my life since leaving school.

'I don't believe it,' he said.

I did not get on very well with the lady in the kiosk. One
morning, I offended her by saying 'What?' and she snarled
back, 'I don't know what you've been taught but I've been
taught "Pardon?" or "I beg your pardon?"'

Back in the cinema, the more friendly Myrtle Eastern
asked me if I could get something down from an upper
shelf – she needed a new light bulb for her tray. 'Oh, what
it is to be tall,' she said. Then she asked if she could go for
her lunch.

'Where do you go?' I asked. 'Down to the pub?'

'Oh no, I just go up to the staff room and have my
sandwiches,' she replied.

I pushed through the red curtains and was watching

Elvis Presley warbling 'Don't You Know I Love you', when suddenly the film broke down. Sounds of frantic rattling and banging came from the projection room.

Later that afternoon, Mr Hill interviewed a new part-time usherette, offered her a job and then invited her to 'stay and watch the film'.

On her first day's work this lady never returned from her tea break.

In the evening, Mr Hill rang her home.

'Oh, I see. Mmmm. Mmmm. No. Well, will you ask her to return the overall? Is she coming back at all? Anyhow, will you ask her to return the overall anyway?'

Mr Hill's life was becoming dreary again when suddenly he entered the office and told me excitedly that George had been seen outside.

'I thought he was in prison,' I said.

'He's been let out early. The police didn't expect him until next week.'

'Have you seen him?'

'No, I haven't seen him. He's been around though.'

'How do you know?'

'The lady in the sweet kiosk told me.'

I saw George a few minutes later. He looked brutal and thwarted, with white froth on his lips. He was standing beside a trolley on which there was a great deal of muddle, including a woman's handbag, bottles of beer and other goods. Then he began to drag his vehicle forward waving people aside with a gloved hand.

'Where does he get the money from in the first place?' I asked Mr Hill.

'He works for it. A copper said he was out there last night serving coffee.'

'What, just after being released?'

'Yeah,' giggled Mr Hill and then after further reflection, 'No, I wouldn't mind hot soup in the winter. That's a good gag. Get George with a big ladle.'

I tried to steer the conversation on to other London characters, past and present, famous and infamous.

'Have you ever heard of John Reginald Halliday Christie?' I asked.

'You what?' replied Mr Hill.

I had been working at the cinema for about four weeks when these routines were disrupted by the arrival of a lady to check the accounts. She was a big woman in a serious black suit and had completely taken over the office. When I entered the room, she said to Mr Hill, 'Who is he?' and when the telephone rang she grabbed it and said, 'Hello – yes?' in an impatient, super-efficient manner.

She also used the telephone to ring Head Office.

'They had their kiosk open well before ten,' she reported.

When I returned from lunch the woman was still there and seemed to take a certain interest when Mr Hill started addressing me rather formally.

'I've just had Head Office on the line,' he said. 'They've decided they don't want your services any longer.'

It took a moment for this news to sink in. Then I asked, 'Do you want me to stay till the end of the day?'

'No, you needn't.'

I did not care to say goodbye to Mr Hill in front of

this unfriendly woman but feeling that I ought to say something, muttered that I would call in and see him again some time.

At this, the lady swung alarmingly into action.

'Why should you want to do that?' she screamed. 'You can come here as a patron, yes, of course, but once you've left the company, you've left the company. You can't come here poking your nose into people's personal affairs.'

'I'm sorry, William,' said Mr Hill, more miserable-looking than ever.

A few minutes later, I was walking down the street with a light step. Near the entrance to the Underground a big poster proclaimed 'Visit Paignton Zoo. Sun, Sands and Scenery. Glorious South Devon.'

I decided to run for a bus, suddenly changed direction and did the splits.

June 1966–April 1969

AT FIRST GLANCE, there was nothing unusual about the café. Its tacked and padded benches could be found anywhere. Then you noticed the posters of famous film stars and the fact that some of the customers were wearing make-up.

'They think I'm God,' said Fred.

Fred was a comedian, a popular figure on the northern club circuit, and the café was one of his haunts when he came to London in search of more sophisticated work. Fred's failure to break through into television was a source of endless annoyance to him. He blamed this on the conservatism of the 'showbiz moguls' and 'the phoney London In Crowd' – yet it impelled him to make regular excursions to the capital. During these visits, Fred and his wife Melody rented a one-room flat in Putney and made frustrating visits to the West End.

'It's just so unbelievable,' said Melody, herself a part-time professional singer. 'Fred always does a bomb.'

After visiting theatrical agents and playing tape recordings of his act, Fred returned to the scenes of his past. Everyone at the café was delighted when he arrived. There were gasps, then laughter, as he mocked and reproved the regular customers.

'Lovely patter, Fred,' said a man named Norman, who had once worked as a female impersonator.

'And that flan you pinched off the counter,' shouted Fred as a trainee ballet dancer was settling his bill.

'Smile at them and they smile back,' Fred said after we'd left. 'They can't afford to offend you.'

Fred had often mentioned his colleague Danny and seemed keen to introduce him to me.

'Danny's had experience,' he explained. 'He's been all over the world. You've got to have suffered to be a comedian.'

'How's Danny?' he asked the next time we visited the café.

'He appeared for a moment yesterday. Otherwise I haven't seen him for weeks,' said the man perched behind the counter.

'Has Danny been in?' Fred asked a few hours later.

'No, I haven't seen the old bag.' The café's owner quickly sprang up, grabbed at a loaf of bread and the ingredients for a salad and began slicing and chopping them with a big knife.

I eventually met Danny Button. He was not an old bag but a small spruce man, a miniature version of Bob Hope. He sailed into the café one afternoon, kissed the waiter and greeted Fred enthusiastically.

Danny was wearing a black mackintosh on top of a white shirt and dark trousers – no jacket.

He sat down beside us. The proprietor shot up and said, 'Gentlemen?' and took our orders.

At first, Danny's hands fiddled while he was speaking but soon he was whispering jokes to Fred and stamping his foot on the floor.

'Isn't it a beautiful, classic line?' he suddenly yelled. 'It sums up the whole of life! All human life is in that line!'

Fred and Danny had met years ago – Fred had spoken with curious sentiment of the time he and Danny shared a flat in London. 'We worked as waiters. We stole food and money. We loafed around – stealing raw sausages and fruit from carts.'

Fred had somehow survived and emerged as a professional entertainer and family man. Danny still lived alone and entirely off his wits.

'Danny is a big baby,' confided the café's proprietor.

The café's proprietor was perhaps thirty when I first met him. A stage-struck but capable young man – his name was Dusty – he wore a pencil behind his ear and held vigorous opinions about current West End shows which he delivered at full pitch all day long.

'It's off next week, darling,' he said of a new production. 'Crummy! They were going to take it off last week. The cast are not sorry. They want to get out of it. It's the biggest load of crap that's ever been conceived.'

When Dusty was not talking about matinées, concert parties, standing ovations or auditions, he was selling his salads, the ingredients for which lay in metal dishes on the counter.

'What salad would you like?' he asked his customers. 'Chicken? Ham? Prawns? Egg mayonnaise? Cream cheese?'

Enquiries about these ingredients were met with, 'It's delicious, I can tell you no more,' and often there were other dishes to recommend.

'I've got a very nice soup on, and a nice light hotpot with vegetables,' he said one evening and then, 'You haven't eaten, William, what can I get you?'

Soon he was holding the bread again and slicing it enthusiastically while talking about the food in other establishments. 'Terrible muck Lyons serve. They're only common peasants. What do you expect?'

'Good business, Dusty?' asked a white-haired man with protruding front teeth.

'Fair. Fair. Hasn't been bad at all.'

Hotpot was then served, the man rubbing his hands together rapidly before beginning to eat, and Dusty turned his attention to the old-fashioned gramophone behind the counter.

Then, against the background of Al Jolson singing, 'How I love you, how I love you,' he began to hold forth about his clientele.

'Most of our customers are in show business or on the fringes of the show business world,' he said.

'What does the waiter do?'

'He wants to be a set designer.'

'My trouble is that I like lying in bed,' said Fred's fan Norman. 'I got up at three this afternoon.'

'Fred will never be out of work,' Dusty continued. 'I think his wife's a very sound influence. She's obviously a pro in every way.'

Sooner or later, the conversation turned to Danny Button.

'Danny's been in the West End for twenty years,' said Dusty.

'Where does he live?'

'In Baker Street. Oh, he has a pretty tough time.'

A few minutes later, he said, 'Danny's on the move. He's a good contact man. He knows people. He's not vegetating.' Then he added, 'Danny's pestered by people who think he's a character.'

'Who was that white-haired man?' I asked.

'Oh, he lives up at Dollis Hill and has a flat in Frinton.'

During these early days I saw quite a lot of Danny and slowly got to know some of the other people who visited the café.

'You come here quite often?' I asked a woman in a white mackintosh and was told, 'Every day.'

'Are you a regular here?' I asked a man with a bright red brass-buttoned waistcoat and shaven neck.

'Regular's a difficult word. Frequent, yes.'

After talking briefly about his life in the army, this man suddenly turned his attention to me.

'You're all coiled up,' he said softly.

Danny Button used the café as an office. He made and received telephone calls there and there was often a letter waiting for him. He knew everyone present and sometimes acted as a master of ceremonies. Some people he dismissed with a phrase: 'He's another disaster, isn't he?' Others he praised highly. A man called Little Joe was, according to Danny, 'the most brilliant boy who comes in here'. Little Joe had short ginger hair and a rubbery, baby-like face on which there was always a certain amount of make-up. He wore a long black braided coat, like a hunting jacket, which fluted out at the back.

Danny invited everyone to test Little Joe's knowledge of the cinema. Someone promptly asked him a question about an elderly character actress called Gladys Henson. 'What was her most famous film?'

'*Derby Day*,' he replied at once.

Little Joe was fond of repeating, 'Talent does what it can. Genius does what it must,' and, 'Most people are failures because they want to be.'

Each time I called at the café, Dusty would fill me in on his customers' latest movements.

'Danny was in on Monday, Wednesday and Thursday.'

'Will Little Joe be in later?'

'He might be, yes.'

Dusty's knife clicked as it hit the enamel top of the fridge, which doubled as a work surface.

'Little Joe has a very high critical faculty,' he continued. 'The trouble is that he had phlebitis at an early age. So unreliable. Loves the night.'

'He works in the theatre, doesn't he?'

'Yes, he dresses.'

The next time I saw Little Joe, he had half a bottle of whisky hidden in a paper bag under the table.

'I'm dressing Wilfred Hyde-White,' he said.

I was slowly becoming aware of the precariousness of these people's lives. One night, Fred and I found Danny half-hidden in a doorway near the café.

'I felt too fucking depressed to go in there,' he said.

'Danny's really suffered,' Fred repeated, 'I feel really sorry for the man. He's often gone without food, cigarettes – he's done moonlight flits. When I'm broke, I just go into a musical show. Danny can't – because he can't sing or dance. He's a funny man. Even you, William, have noticed that.'

Fred and I had met the previous year in Manchester where I had gone a few months after leaving school in a bid to enter the entertainment business myself. The bid had eventually come to nothing – no one has ever laughed at my jokes – but one of the good things that had come out of the experience was my meeting with Fred, a real professional capable of handling an audience of five hundred people and generating tumultuous applause. Now, through him, I had been introduced to a strange café where conversation endlessly revolved around show business matters.

'She wants to do comedy stuff. *Castle in the Air* she was superb,' said Dusty.

'She was diabolical when I saw her,' said one of the waiters.

'Look what Hollywood said about her. Wouldn't let her in the door,' said Norman.

'She's a brilliant end-of-pier revue artiste,' insisted Little Joe.

Guffaws and bursts of applause greeted these judgements which were sometimes followed by comments on struggling actors among the café's clientele.

'He could have had *Salad Days*,' said Dusty. 'He wishes he'd taken it now. He refused it because he thought it was too tat.'

'What he can do is sue for loss of wages,' he said of another customer. 'That boy could be in America now.'

Early that summer, Fred forsook this world and went north to fulfil some long-standing engagements. In his absence, I tried to stay in touch with Danny but he kept his distance. Once I saw him hurrying away from the café just as I arrived. Another time I heard he had appeared just after I'd left.

'He's an elusive old hag,' said Dusty.

Apparently I wasn't the only person interested in him. His name was often on people's lips. One afternoon a black man carrying a musical instrument in a case entered the café and asked, 'Is Danny Button here?'

'Everyone's looking for Danny Button,' said Dusty.

I chatted instead to the white-haired man with protruding teeth. In a soft voice, he asked me if I knew the tartans and, if so, did I know the MacNab? Then he slid along the bench towards a Scotchman in a woolly jumper and began talking about a recent Royal Variety Show in which the Beatles had appeared.

'John Lennon's crack, "Don't applaud, just rattle your jewellery," I thought that was damn funny,' said the white-haired man.

Later his companion started talking slowly and sentimentally about his home town, Kirkcaldy.

'When the spring tides are on and the esplanade's flooded you get sandbags all along the front.'

Then Little Joe arrived. He looked spruce in his black

coat. While drinking soup, he suddenly paused to offer me a cigarette. Later – he worked partly as a waiter – he started making a salad for me. 'What shall I give you as a base?' he asked.

His movements in the kitchen were hurried and decisive. When a pastry got knocked off the counter, he flipped it into the waste-bin without a thought.

Little Joe and I then discussed the Alfred Hitchcock film *Marnie* which was showing at the cinema where I was now working. Little Joe told me that the screenplay was by Jay Presson Allen, 'who also adapted *Prime of Miss Jean Brodie*'. The music was by Bernard Herrmann 'who studied under Klemperer' and was 'his finest score'. The controversial backcloth in the film was deliberately used by the director 'to emphasize the unreality of the situation' and 'the moment of revelation, as in all Hitchcock's films, comes in the lavatory'.

I later asked him if he had seen Danny Button and he replied, 'The last time I saw Danny Button, he was feeling rather blue.'

When I paid my bill, Dusty whispered, 'Danny's run off with someone's wife. That's why he's been lying low.'

Then he added excitedly, 'Someone's going to kill the Button.'

The café was at its most chaotic in the middle of the evening, when Dusty and whoever was assisting him were hard at work preparing trays of tea, coffee, sandwiches and salads and then delivering them backstage at theatres across the West End. 'We do every theatre, bar two,' Dusty had explained. 'We don't do the Duchess and we don't do the

Old Vic.' Now at seven o'clock one summer evening, Dusty was cursing and shouting out the names of food and theatres.

'Take that down to the New. Get a cab. Tea and trifle for the man you don't like . . . Fucking Comedy! Is sugar in? Fruit salads for room eleven. They've ordered coffee as well. They've got their own sugar.'

These dramas were constantly interrupted by the telephone ringing with further orders or alterations to orders.

'Leslie Phillips's dressing-room want two chicken and tomato sandwiches immediately.'

One evening at this hour, Dusty ignored me as he left the premises with a covered tray, and when I sat down at one of the tables, Little Joe told me, 'We're closed.'

When the fuss was over, Dusty returned to his café walking like a tired horse, and there was a brief post-mortem – 'A forty-minute fuck-up at the Globe' – and further cries of, 'This fucking evil Saturday.'

Then Dusty would mop his brow, make himself a pot of tea and declare, 'Half an hour's peace.'

Late at night, when the theatres had finished and heavily loaded Covent Garden lorries began to thunder past the window, the café filled up again. The door was now bolted and heavy red curtains blocked in all the light so that from the street the place looked closed. Prospective customers rang a buzzer and sometimes waited a long time before the door was opened. When they had got in, the bolts were shot home again, creating an atmosphere of privacy and security.

'I hope this is interesting,' said Dusty when the buzzer went one night.

It was Norman, currently working as a cloak-room attendant at the Lyric Theatre. He pushed his way through the curtains which also enveloped the door, his face as pale as death, his sandy hair as neat as it could possibly be.

'A year and a day I do declare,' said Dusty, though less than a week had passed since Norman's last visit.

The former female impersonator was soon settled on one of the long padded benches that faced each other from both sides of the café. He nodded in all directions, screwing up his eyes then laughing, smiling and involving everyone in his glances.

'I'll have a coffee when you're ready, Dusty,' he said, then, 'You haven't got a crust of granary out there, have you?'

Everyone watched Norman eat this late snack and his eyes followed each speaker as the conversation turned again to show business.

'A very drawn-out type of production, *Camelot*, wasn't it?' he said eventually.

'One of the best presses ever,' said Dusty of a show that had just opened. 'Even the hardened professionals are raving about it.'

'The music is such heaven you're won over immediately,' added the waiter on duty.

'I hope they make a film of it,' said Little Joe.

At about two-thirty in the morning, Norman left, remarking that he wanted to get 'a nice early night', and

the circle broke up. In a corner, a foppish pair – the younger
man looked like a cow – began deliberating over their
plans: 'Shall we go, love?' and 'I hate to remind you but
we've got a bus to catch.' When Dusty eventually saw this
couple out and shot the bolt home after them he muttered,
'Too much!' as he straightened the tables and chairs.

Dusty then put on a record of Fred Astaire singing,
'Night and day, you are the one. Only you beneath the
moon and under the sun.'

Just as I was waiting to pay one afternoon in July, Danny
swept into the café at high speed. He quickly tore up two
bills which were waiting for him and began to crack jokes.
His teeth gleamed white as he asked, 'Is there any need to
wear mink underwear in this weather?' and then, spotting
me, 'Are you still living with Albert Hall?' Later, he glided
about the café trying out further bits of patter, picking up
dirty plates and rallying the other customers to share his
notions.

'Wouldn't William make a good Richard Three?' he
asked.

His ebullience knew no bounds. 'I've just written
eight tellies for Roy Castle,' he announced – and met the
murmurs of disbelief with counter cries of 'Enemy!' and
'Liar!'

I tried to steer the conversation into literary topics
asking if he had read any of the works of George Eliot, but
he stifled this line of enquiry by replying, 'I wrote them
all.'

Finally, he allowed me to see a new contract he had
obtained and the cause of his high spirits. 'Try not to tear

it,' he said, grabbing the document back and setting off again saying, 'Bye-bye, William. Bye-bye, Dusty.'

Dusty then announced to the whole café, 'Danny's fixed himself up some dates in Blackpool. He goes up there tomorrow.'

The next day, I spotted Fred in Charing Cross Road – and he immediately began raging against the theatrical establishment. 'You've met me at an interesting time,' he said. 'I've just been playing through some tapes of my act and they show me to be, without doubt, the greatest entertainer in this country.'

He went on to describe a new comedian, with his own television show, as 'a complete amateur, a sham and an idiot'.

In the café, Dusty was also in an agitated state. 'This agent's doing his nut. Eight times he's been on the phone from Blackpool. Danny's sent a telegram saying he's ill. The agent seems such a nice person. Can't get a replacement. He's rung Danny's home twice and he's not there, so he can't be ill.'

'He's frightened,' said Fred, drawing on a cigarette.

'That's your answer,' said Norman. 'Danny's not what you call a knock-about comedian, is he?'

The following evening, Fred asked, 'Did Danny go north?' and Dusty replied, 'No, he was in tonight.'

'He's frightened of success,' Fred continued. 'One big occasion and he goes to pieces.'

'Danny doesn't like to work,' said Dusty. 'He's not interested in the profession.'

Fred was now in a rather better mood as he had just been booked to appear at a famous new club in Liverpool called The Flamingo and noted, Fred said, for its pear-shaped stage extending into the audience.

A few days later, I found Danny alone in the café. He looked so grim that at first I did not recognize him. He sat in a corner with a look of pain and unease contorting his face. As I approached him, I noticed a half-eaten trifle in front of him, and on the seat beneath him, a newspaper was rucked up. Not until I was very close was I certain it was him. I tried to be friendly but he looked at me resentfully. When I asked him if he had seen Fred, he replied in a low voice, 'Don't talk to me about him. I'm not interested.'

He then champed his jaws together and ran his tongue over his lips.

'Has Fred told you he's only been doing comedy for the last eighteen months?' he asked. 'He tells that to everybody. He's been doing comedy for eighteen years. Fred is such a liar.'

'Show business is a business,' he continued. 'It's got to work. You've got to be a yes-man. Fred'll leave show business. Show business does not like characters. Or eccentrics. Or geniuses. It likes businesslike people.'

From the next table the Young Fop sat with his chin in his hand, and a fat signet ring on his finger, making eyes at us – and everyone else in the café.

'He's had it,' said Danny, glancing away in even greater pain. 'He's a homosexual.'

There was always some drama in the café. Current films and

West End productions were torn to shreds. Famous figures were cut down to size or puffed up beyond comprehension.

'Of course Dora Bryan's a dear to work with,' said Dusty one evening. 'Mary Martin's an absolute pig.'

Norman clapped his hands and said, 'But the public change, dear.'

'For Christ's sake,' said Dusty from the kitchen, 'if Bette Davis is going to play in a straight play, let her play in a good one.'

'They're not going to change the formula now,' he said a few minutes later. 'Elvis needs Paramount Pictures more than they need him.'

Danny's depression had lifted enough for him to chip in with his own pronouncements about figures closer to home – 'Margaret Rutherford's the biggest liberty-taker in show business,' then, 'Wisdom's films nearly always make a million' – and Little Joe soon surprised everybody by declaring, 'Julie Andrews is the sexiest woman in films.'

Norman seemed to prefer to reminisce about figures from the remote past. 'D'you remember when they interviewed Hedy Lamarr on the set of *The Flesh is Weak*, Dusty?'

Dusty was equally well-informed about forthcoming productions and the arrival in London of any big international celebrities.

'Thank God we've got a star here next week. The one and only Miss Marlene Dietrich.'

Late one summer night, just after midnight, a young couple with a sleeping baby entered the café. They explained that they had been scouring London all evening, desperate for accommodation.

'Clapham, Balham, we've just missed an unfurnished three-room flat in Balham.'

'How much can you afford?' asked the white-haired man with protruding teeth.

'About five pounds ten if it was biggish.'

'What about the baby?'

'She's fifteen months and no trouble.'

'Have you tried Whitechapel?' somebody suggested.

'D'you mean Cable Street?' Little Joe then asked this questioner with some alarm.

The woman then set off on another errand, leaving the man with the sleeping baby on his lap to face further questioning from the white-haired man. 'How old are you?' 'Twenty-eight.' 'What are you working at?' 'Casual driver.' 'Ever been in trouble?' 'No,' sighed the man. 'I'm an actor, you see.'

The woman then returned and immediately addressed the baby.

'Hello, how did you wake up?' To the man she said, 'Any luck? Doesn't Dusty know anywhere?'

The café's proprietor was out at the time – he had been given tickets for a Marlene Dietrich concert – and returned a few minutes after the couple had left. I noticed he was wearing his usual grey trousers but had put on a clean white shirt, a blazer and a yellow tie. He was in a state of excitement.

'She came on wearing a cloak of chain-mail, which she took off after four numbers. She did "Accustomed to his Face" and the place fell down. She was camping it up the entire time. She looked daggers at the conductor twice.

There was twenty minutes of applause at the end . . . She was crying . . .'

The homeless couple's troubles were temporarily eclipsed but they must have made contact with Dusty later because a notice soon went up announcing, 'Wanted urgently. One large room unfurnished.'

Several times during the next few days the homeless man made brief appearances at the café. Dusty greeted him warmly, supplied him with florentines and other unsuitable food from the counter which he took out to the car where the mother and baby were waiting.

At last they found a flat somewhere – a rent of eighty-five shillings a week was mentioned – and the homeless man used the telephone in the café to make the arrangements. The girl stood beside him giggling.

I had now left the cinema and was looking for a job in advertising. After interviews, I would sometimes drop in at the café at tea-time and be surprised to find it populated by decent-looking women reading light novels, their faces wincing into a smile when they came to a funny bit – or chatting among themselves about the identity of the film stars depicted in the posters on the café's walls. 'I imagine that'll be Joan Crawford.'

Other customers appeared more high-powered. One afternoon, a small foreign lady said, 'A tea please, Dusty, as I'm going out to dinner,' and Dusty said later, 'That was Petronelle, the American ballet mistress. She's in London auditioning for the TV series, *Dance of the Queen Bee*.'

Another afternoon, I was surprised to find Fred's wife Melody chatting to Dusty. Her hair was swept up above her head like pineapple leaves and secured with a red ribbon.

We talked briefly about Fred, now moving about the north country again, and about Melody's own career as a singer. Afterwards Dusty declared, 'She's obviously a fully trained soprano.'

Sometimes these discussions were disturbed by the arrival of a delivery man from the Merrie Miller bakeries, who asked, 'Is there a bloke here called Dusty?' or by some incident outside. One afternoon, Dusty re-entered the café remarking, 'Lots of blokes with banners coming up the street.'

Dusty used the lull in activity to talk about himself – his favourite subjects at school had been 'English and Theatricals' – or to warn his assistants about the pressure ahead, 'In case you're busy here – see what I mean?' and then, 'In ten days' time, we'll be so busy we won't be able to walk.'

Sometimes the telephone rang, Dusty picked it up and said quietly, 'Oh, hello, Danny.'

At night, the atmosphere was less sedate. One evening the door crashed open and a bedraggled young man with blood around his mouth stumbled into a seat beside me. This would-be customer was gently removed by Dusty's wiry arm and coaxing, 'All right, m'dear.'

Another evening, I arrived to find a large elderly man with no socks on and all his washing things, including a toothbrush, spread out on a table. He appeared better educated, more patrician, than the rest of the clientele – an exile from Chelsea or Fulham Road.

'I've just been having a small glass of sherry with Sybil

Thorndike and Sir Lewis Casson,' he boomed. 'I wonder if
Dusty would let me sleep on the floor?'

His name was Humphrey. He had been an actor of
some sort, and was now in a pickle. Soon he was boasting
of his familiarity with Noël Coward – 'Noël looks too
Chinese' – and latching on to anybody who would talk to
him and conceivably offer shelter for the night.

'What's your address – for Christmas cards and
things?' he asked me. Then, 'You must come to one of my
Thursday evenings in Brighton.'

When his request to sleep on the floor was politely
refused, he shuffled off, saying, 'It's all right. I'll spend the
night with one of my four hundred boyfriends. They're all
longing to see me.'

After he'd left, Dusty described this man as 'the
craftiest old sod in London – most people would detour
three miles to avoid him.'

'Oh, he's awful,' said Danny. 'Such a queen.'

That autumn, Danny seemed to re-emerge as the star of the
café and the ring-master of its events. He threw his weight
about, commented on new arrivals – 'These loungers will
go in a moment . . . hey, this is naughty' – and even cast
judgement on my own stability: 'I think you could become
a bit neurotic later on, William.'

He also mocked Dusty's theatrical ambitions merci-
lessly. 'Dusty, get your drag!' he yelled. 'Oooh, the lights!
They're still waiting!'

In a lower voice, he murmured, 'Dusty's a terrific guy
actually.'

When I asked him if he had seen Fred, he replied,

'Fred is dead! He died in Nottingham clutching a photograph of me!'

One night I called at the café after midnight and found Dusty, Little Joe and a waiter gathered round the counter playing a game with paper and pencils. Sitting alone at a table near the door was the man called Humphrey. As the night wore on, he began casting increasingly furious glances in the direction of three girls who were gossiping in another corner.

'I can't bear this twittering and fluttering,' he began.

The girls guessed that he was referring to their chatter and there was a burst of resentful murmuring.

Humphrey then leaned forward in his seat and peered at the girls with exaggerated interest. His brow was knitted and his eyes had a look of horrified attention.

'What are you doing?' he asked in a much fiercer voice. 'What are you doing?' he repeated the question even more indignantly. Then he pointed an accusing finger at one of the girls. 'Go to the ladies' room!' he shouted.

Dusty's group at the counter had remained frozen, but at this last remark Little Joe spluttered as he tried to control his laughter.

Then one of the girls broke the silence. 'Shut up, you silly old man. She's only doing her belt. Why shouldn't she do her belt?'

Dusty left his perch and swept down the café to remove my plate and take a further order. He was pretending nothing had happened. The old man returned to his salad muttering – and there was a general feeling of relief.

'This place has changed,' said one of the girls later. 'I'm not coming again if that man is here.'

'Well, I shall be gone in the spring,' said Dusty. 'I'm after a less exacting position.'

At lunch-time, the café's tables were laid out in advance with knives, spoons, forks, paper napkins and tumblers. The clientele were smarter and more successful than the evening crowd – antiquarian book dealers from Charing Cross Road, and British Museum employees in flapping well-cut suits. Conversation sometimes reached rarefied heights unthinkable in the evening.

'I sat next to him at Boodle's the other night,' said a senior antiquarian. 'He was just a lee-tle unsure of himself.'

Wearing a corduroy cap and holding his smile for a long time, Dusty served these people lunch. He offered the same range of food as he served in the evening and encouraged everyone to have three courses. 'Soup and bread? What salad would you like? Chicken? Ham? Egg mayonnaise? Cream cheese?' was followed by a choice of desserts. 'Chocolate rum slice? Belgian apple? Fresh fruit salad? Florentine? There's strawberry trifle with cream if you'd prefer.' There was no time for conversation on these occasions but to customers he knew well, Dusty would sometimes remark, 'I'm getting out of here.'

My own attempts at small talk at this time of day were far from welcome.

'You're mad,' shouted Dusty one lunch-time. 'As mad as a hatter.'

In the evening, the conversation became mildly flattering or self-mocking. Dusty conceded that there was money in madness. He also unveiled more ambitious plans for himself

– 'In two years' time I shall be a star!' Later, Norman acted out a tiff with a patron at the theatre where he now worked as a cloakroom attendant.

'What is this I see? A cashmere coat all creased and wet? And what is this? Has it been on the floor?' Norman had replied evasively, 'Granted this is a gorgeous raincoat. You probably paid what for it?'

The daintiness of these talks was to be disturbed by a series of interruptions by the man named Humphrey. The old man could not keep away from the café and was soon making further trouble, bulldozing into everybody's conversations, dropping names. 'I'm an old tramp . . . you're very lucky to see me at all . . . somebody dropped a lobster on my foot . . . a former lover of mine . . . his wife, his boyfriend . . . my stepson . . . Cassius Clay . . . Princess Margaret . . . silly publicity . . . my grandson, my godson . . .'

Soon a row developed between him and Little Joe – the young man had imitated his voice.

'Don't try to send me up like that,' shouted the old man. 'You look like something out of an insect opera.'

'You're not well, Humphrey,' Danny shouted back on Little Joe's behalf.

After the man had left, somebody asked, 'What does the guy do?'

Danny said with a sigh of resignation, 'He's a moron,' and others present tried to console the boy who had been insulted.

'I've forgotten him already,' said Little Joe with a dismissive flap of his hand.

'Just another enemy he's made,' added Danny.

These visits by the old man had repercussions, however, and I heard people brooding about him several days
later. 'That bloke makes me sick . . . so evil . . . so rude . . .
That Humphrey, oh, he's horrible . . . Isn't he boring? Isn't
he dreadful?'

There was also talk about a mackintosh the old man
had left behind. 'Tatty thing,' said Dusty. 'I wouldn't wrap
a dog in it.'

The next time I called at the café, there were dozens of
Christmas cards on the walls – and the café's popular owner
was clinging momentarily to a pole which supported part
of the ceiling.

'Now, children,' he began.

The telephone rang and Dusty said, 'Oh no. Not
again. Go to hell!' and when it started again he screamed,
'Piss off!'

Soon tuna fish salads were going into paper bags. 'In a
cab! Her Majesty's salads!' Dusty ordered the baggy-
trousered girl who was helping him.

'Should I go now?'

'Yes, you're late already!'

Dusty looked smaller and thinner. His hand touched
his hair and then his ear and then his tongue went into his
cheek as he deliberated over which delivery should come
next.

When things had calmed down again, Little Joe asked
me, 'What are you doing on Christmas Day?' and I asked
Dusty, 'Has anyone dropped out of the scene?'

'Humphrey.'

'Where's he gone?'

'Don't know. Nobody knows.'

On Christmas Eve, I called at the café again and found Dusty serious and tense, zipping up a suitcase and telling his new assistant, 'There's half a bottle of wine in the fridge if you want it.'

'Has anyone seen Danny Button?' I asked when I returned to the café early in January.

'I saw him on Boxing Day,' volunteered Little Joe.

Danny's foot tapped nervously on the leg of my chair when we met that evening.

'No, actually, I wanted to see you,' he said.

I told him I had spent Christmas in a remote village in the West Country.

'You haven't been working as a comic down there?'

I told him I had abandoned show business and now had a job in advertising – the office was just down the road.

'Any good?'

I said the people were a bit boring.

'Squares, aren't they?' he agreed.

Then he said, 'I saw Fred.'

'How is he?'

'He just said he was working.'

Times were bad for Danny. He was making ends meet by helping Dusty with the theatre deliveries. One evening I found him kneeling on the floor wiping up spilt cream – and then bouncing and loping past the window carrying a tray of food, his head muffled up with a scarf.

Later, when he was back at his usual seat near the till, I started boasting that I was working on a television commercial involving the comedian Billy Dainty.

'Don't make me vomit while I'm having my tea,' he said quietly.

Early in the New Year, the café's regulars were joined by an old woman in black. She had few teeth but spoke in a refined voice, smoked Turkish cigarettes and mentioned her 'family solicitor' in a dismissive manner. Her name was Miss Fox. She was Jewish, had lodgings in Bloomsbury and worked as a second-hand book dealer.

'Where's my Joe?' she asked on her second and third visit. The old lady had taken a fancy to the young film buff.

'He's on holiday,' said Dusty.

'Where's he gone?'

'Nowhere.'

'Where's the waiter?' I asked.

'Off-duty. I don't know where he is.'

The café was also suffering from the lull. 'Bye-bye, Dusty,' said the girl who was helping him with deliveries, thumping out, altering the position of three chairs and protesting, 'Whoops! Clumsy me! I must knock the table, mustn't I?'

Later I heard Dusty saying, 'Money generally is getting very tight. We're being taxed out of existence.'

Miss Fox was soon to be found at the café every night, from seven o'clock to midnight and beyond. Her special cigarettes gave the premises a sophisticated smell and her all-black costume, black hat and black framed spectacles added a new element to the visual scene. Night after night, she sat in the same window seat, chain-smoking her cigarettes and squashing their ends into the floor beneath the seat from which she never moved in the course of an evening.

From time to time, I chose a place beside her and we would discuss books and writers. 'C. S. Lewis was frightfully keen on George Macdonald,' she told me in melting tones.

These intimacies were too much for Danny and he was soon shouting from the other end of the café, 'When are you going to Bravingtons, William?'

Behind his counter, Dusty ignored this jibe and concentrated on cutting up ingredients for a salad. Occasionally, he waltzed down the café to take an order or answer the doorbell — a new two-tone chime had been installed — let in new customers and shoot the bolts home.

Finally, late at night, the click of Dusty's kitchen knife was replaced by the sound of coins being dropped into plastic cups. As he cashed up, he started humming to himself, 'Strangers in the Night . . .'

Considerable rejoicing greeted Dusty's announcement that 'the old sod Humphrey' was now in prison. The revelation was followed by widespread regret that he was only serving a fourteen-day sentence.

On his release, the old man immediately reappeared at the café and asked, 'Have you ever been in gaol, Dusty?'

Dusty did not reply to this question, which was followed by another impertinence.

'May I draw you in the nude, Dusty?'

'Not at this time,' replied the café's owner gracefully.

Danny, meanwhile, was suffering from a bad cold. One night I found him sitting bolt upright in a corner seat. His mackintosh was buttoned round his neck and strapped tightly in, exaggerating the size of his bottom.

'Coffee?' I offered him.

'No, thanks – you go ahead.'

'Florentine?'

'It's all right. I've had seventeen already.'

His lips looked burnt out and his mackintosh smelled of café fry-ups. Danny patronized other establishments beside this one, where smellier food was served.

'Anything exciting happened?' I asked.

'I'm alive.'

I laughed too loudly at this reply and he said, 'Hey, take it easy on the nerves.'

Soon Miss Fox entered wearing a shiny black sou'wester. 'Sensible hat for this weather,' remarked Norman.

Then Little Joe set off with a tray of coffees and teas. I watched him through the window as he darted between different doorways with his burden.

Danny remained wrapped in gloom. Then he said solemnly, 'Comedians are useless people. They're a luxury.'

I asked him if he had seen his old colleague.

'I don't think Fred is working as a comic now.'

I glanced at him and he returned my glance and then turned away shutting his eyes, filling his cheeks with air and blowing out.

When I looked at him again I saw for the first time that he was wearing false eyelashes.

I eventually acquired a new telephone number for Fred. He was back in the city where I had first met him two years earlier.

'How's Manchester?' I asked.

'At my feet,' he said but his voice sounded quavery, bleak and weary, full of unshed tears. A child was crying in the background.

Then he said, 'I'm coming down on Monday and have no plans from then on.'

The following week, I was sitting in the café after work when I heard a familiar snort in the doorway.

'Hello, me old flower,' said Fred.

My friend was wearing the same blue suit that he often wore on the stage but I noticed there was now a tiny, neat patch on the knee.

'I'm in a state of half-slumber at the moment,' he said, eyeing the occupants of the next table and then launching into his usual invective about the show business establishment.

'All I want is recognition. By the Delfonts et cetera. I haven't even got past the lower strata of agents.'

He began boasting that his jokes were constantly being stolen by well-known stars – some of whom, he was absolutely certain, sent spies to cover his club appearances. He also claimed that a young comedian was borrowing his name – 'I suppose just to get himself a few Welsh working men's audiences.'

Over coffee and pastries, he said, 'I've even started

worrying about the food and the rent again, which of course
is ridiculous.'

When we parted company, he said, 'If you see Danny,
wish him well from me.'

That night at the café, Danny questioned me closely
about his old friend. 'Has Fred still got his car? Oh, I'm
glad Fred has sold his car – because Fred is blind, you know
... Fred'll leave show business ... Fred looks a million
years old now. I look better than him, don't I? Don't I?'

After a while, he began to speak more affectionately of
the time when the two of them had shared a flat. 'Fred
would suddenly go out and buy ten pounds worth of
groceries. He was that sort of person.'

Then he added, 'Fred was a chorus boy in *Kiss Me
Kate*,' and, 'I haven't seen his act for years.'

Our conversation was halted when two real stars,
currently appearing together in a new West End musical,
entered the café. Dusty sailed up to their table, took orders
for salads and then said apologetically, 'I've only got enough
cream cheese for one.' He got on well with the actress, best
known for her love affair with one of the Beatles, but
seemed uneasy with the young actor.

After this couple had left, Dusty praised the show in
which they were appearing. 'It's packed. You can't get in.
It's block-booked. They're booking into October.'

The following afternoon the young actor was again in
the café, this time accompanied by his wife, mother,
grandmother and several children. When he eventually paid
his bill, there was a sad expression on Dusty's face.

'Dusty's on equal terms with so many stars,' said
Norman later.

He was also a rock of security in many less fortunate people's lives. Many people – myself included – looked upon the café as a haven. Once I heard a girl using the telephone saying, 'I'm down at Dusty's. Tell me mum I'm all right.'

Though strict with his customers – 'It's no good ranting and roaring like a third-rate child' – Dusty had their best interests at heart. 'Little Joe's in bed,' he announced one evening. 'Skin swelling around his legs and face. An allergy.'

A few days later, he added, 'Doctor has insisted Little Joe does not get drunk.'

He was also a source of practical help. One afternoon I heard him explaining to someone about box-office work, tearing tickets. 'Enquire at Her Majesty's stage door. They used to do their front-of-house from there. Enquire there. They'll tell you who the woman is.'

One summer evening, I heard Miss Fox whisper, 'I wanted a word with you, Dusty.' The proprietor immediately slipped into a seat beside her and the two were then closeted in conversation. I heard the old lady say, 'I've been evicted,' and then, 'Could I really?' and I gathered she needed a place for her old books and Dusty was agreeing to store them for her.

'Put the valuable ones in there,' he said, indicating a cubby-hole behind the counter. 'Stack them in a little pile. Put the other ones out in the yard under the canopy.'

'Thanks awfully,' said Miss Fox.

Dusty then appealed to all those present for temporary lodgings for the old lady herself. 'Does anyone know where our dear madam could roost for a few days, a few weeks?'

The café was a bright corner in many people's lives – and when that August Dusty closed the place for ten days to go on a package holiday to Portugal with a friend, the café's regulars were lost souls again. Miss Fox alone remained on the premises – she had temporarily moved into the windowless cellar below the café – the others were scattered across London. One afternoon, I saw Little Joe running through the colourful crowds in King's Road, Chelsea, his black jacket flying out at the back. A few days later, I saw him in the Leicester Square reference library, concentrating hard on a film magazine. Another day I saw one of the waiters pushing a bicycle up Whitehall and one night I saw Danny Button, a more resourceful figure, pushing open the door of a block of flats in Great Newport Street.

'I thoroughly enjoyed it! A wonderful rest!' said Dusty on his return. Then he added, 'I lost weight on holiday. I perspire the earth.'

The telephone was ringing again. 'Shut up and go away!' screamed Dusty and everyone was back in their normal places. Over by the door Miss Fox looked none the worse for her nights in the cellar and was playing chess with her friend Little Joe. 'Check,' she said in her leisurely voice, and then giggled mischievously and drew on her Turkish cigarette. 'Want another?' she asked almost the moment the game was finished.

I then noticed that a new figure had joined the regulars. He wore a brown overcoat with a brown velvet collar, spit-and-polished boots and – in spite of the summer weather – scarf and gloves. Slow-moving, dignified and with a chiselled face, he bore a superficial resemblance to the Duke of Edinburgh. He had a library book propped open on the table-top and his gloves carefully arranged beside it.

'Who was that strange man?' I asked later.

Dusty replied that the new customer was simply 'methodical' and after a short pause asked, 'Why do you hate everybody?'

Early in October I was queuing during the lunch hour at the National Gallery canteen when a voice said, 'One tea, one coffee,' but I did not immediately recognize it. Suddenly I found Danny standing beside me. He was as astonished as I was and immediately proclaimed that I had been following him. When he raised his hand to a black woman behind the counter and she said, 'Hi, Danny!' I realized that this was another of his favourite haunts.

With Danny was a small blonde girl whom I had occasionally seen in the café.

During the next few weeks, Danny and his new friend – her name was Miss Smith – made innumerable appearances at the café. Occasionally I joined them at the table where they sat close together, hand in hand.

The progress of the romance was carefully charted by Dusty. 'Mr Button's at the movies with his girlfriend,' said Dusty one evening. 'They'll be here in a moment.'

Later, Danny and the girl rushed into the café hand in hand, stood for a moment at the counter and then rushed out past me. Miss Smith's face seemed to be all screwed up and she was hustling her boyfriend on.

'Say nothing,' she hissed. 'Say absolutely nothing.'

A few days later a more unpleasant encounter took place.

'You're a great big bullshitter,' Miss Smith suddenly shouted at me. 'You're typical of everything I can't stand!'

On this occasion, Danny smiled at me apologetically but the following day he said, 'Go away, William. Don't go on. I'm not interested. Sit over there.'

I was stung by these hostilities but relieved to learn that I was not the only cause of Danny's distress.

'He was in twice yesterday,' said the proprietor a few days later. 'In a very funny mood. Wouldn't talk to anybody. This girl is insisting he marries her. He was in again this evening, looking very worried.'

For a few hours, a rumour circulated that Danny had given his girlfriend a ring but before the end of the week, Dusty was able to announce that the affair was over.

'Miss Smith was in having a salad. No, they don't speak.'

The following day, Danny responded in a more normal fashion to a question about Fred.

'Dead!' he replied. 'Strangled by an ant in Huddersfield!'

'Did you have a nice summer?' asked Little Joe. It seemed a strange question to ask in the middle of November.

Then he said, 'What can I buy you? Coffee? A meal?'

He was wearing the same black hunting coat that he had worn when I first met him, though some of the braid was now missing.

'I'm not well,' he said. 'I'm a complete nonentity. I know nothing about anything. I have no application.'

I suggested that he might earn a living as a writer but he replied that this would be 'beyond all dreams'. Writing, he said, was only 'an interesting pastime'.

'How about copywriting?' I asked, thinking that my current occupation might suit him.

'Oh, I've never been one for the neat turn of phrase,' he replied.

Our conversation ended on another odd note. 'I'm thinking of taking up rugby next season,' he said.

Fred had not been strangled by an ant in Huddersfield but had made his first step into the Big Time. When we met by chance in Charing Cross Road at the end of November, Fred told me he had been discovered by a new talent scout and been booked to appear on a television variety show which would be broadcast the following week. 'He's holding me out of clubs at the moment,' said Fred of his new manager.

'Well, at least one of your customers is doing well,' I told Dusty later.

'Who?'

'I'm not telling.'

Dusty guessed who I was talking about and said, 'Fred always does well. He'll never be out of work. I wish someone could do the same for the Button.'

Fred was to appear on television several times that winter and when we met again in the spring he was in a new sheepskin coat, leather boots and sharply creased sky-blue trousers. As was his wont, he had just been to see

Danny to share with him his good luck – but had found his friend dejected.

'He's lost a stone in weight. It must be something to do with his private life.'

Since breaking up with Miss Smith, Danny had tried to avoid the café but I continued to catch glimpses of him in the West End. One afternoon, I saw him in Leicester Square near a shop that sold stage make-up, his coat collar turned up against the wind. Another day I saw him alone in the pub near my office, skirting the crowds at the bar, moving fast.

One morning, on my way to work, I passed him on the pavement, red-faced and sore. He blinked when he saw me but made no other sign of recognition.

I was surprised, therefore, when, soon after this last encounter, the telephone rang in my office and Danny's voice came through disturbingly loud and clear. 'I wanted to get in touch with Fred rather urgently,' he said. 'Do you know where he is this week?'

The following morning, Danny suddenly appeared in person at my place of work.

'I'm going up to Sunderland for three months,' he said, leaning through the office door smiling. 'Fred said to come and see you.'

He had had his hair cut and was once again the Bob Hope figure that I had first admired but his face was thinner and there were dark rings under his eyes.

Curiously, he seemed more concerned about my own appearance. 'You don't look too well, William,' he said.

A second and equally unexpected meeting took place an hour later when I left the building at lunch-time. Danny suddenly materialized and asked immediately to borrow money from me.

'I was expecting a cheque this morning. I'll pay you back as soon as I get straight.'

He quickly pocketed a few pounds and picked up a suitcase which he had cheekily left with my firm's commissionaire.

'Right,' I said. 'Good luck.'

'Don't go – you're not free yet.'

Danny insisted that I walk with him to the café. He bounced along confidently, toes pointing inwards. Suddenly two fire-engines hurtled by. Moments later, they roared past us in the opposite direction. 'They're back,' said Danny. 'It was a false alarm.'

The café was crowded but we squeezed in beside some antique dealers. Danny chose a pasty and sweetcorn and spoke optimistically about his trip to the north-east, where Fred, now appearing in a leading night-club, had invited Danny to join him.

'Apparently Fred is working very well,' he said.

A few days later I returned to the café after work and found Dusty in an animated state.

'Mr Button has returned to London.'

Before he could explain more, the telephone rang and Dusty's attention was diverted to more pressing matters as various old faithfuls began to arrive. The first was Norman, perfectly groomed, pampered and deathly pale as ever.

'Dusty, d'you think I could have a tomato sandwich in white bread?' he whispered.

'Yes, surely,' said Dusty.

At her usual hour in sneaked Miss Fox, carrying three books. She got herself some coffee and a glass of water and took her usual seat alongside an unfamiliar middle-aged man – the café still attracted passing trade – who said he was taking the train to Fort William that night.

Dusty pounded about the café – slap went his plimsolls on the badly cracked lino – satisfying his customers. Then, jobs done and pans scrubbed out, he swung into a seat beside me.

'Danny's opening at the Astor Club, he says.'

The next time I saw Fred – his new chunky haircut made him look rather tame – he said he was fed up with his old colleague.

'Button's little ways. I'm completely finished with the man.'

While Dusty fussed around us, Fred talked briefly about his own career – 'I've got so much work piling up, it's ridiculous' – and about his life in general. 'I'm bored on the domestic front,' he said. A few minutes later, he said, 'Excuse me while I make a telephone call. I'm just arranging my overnight accommodation.'

The same night, I met Danny himself and we talked for a while about neutral topics. Then he asked in a leering voice, 'Any news of him?'

I said I had heard nothing.

'Fred is going a little bit insane,' Danny volunteered hopefully.

Dusty had further news for me when I paid my bill.

'Norman hasn't been in the theatre all week. They're going mental.'

A few days later, I arrived at the café to find Little Joe, Dusty and Danny huddled round the counter. On the edge of the group was the man who resembled the Duke of Edinburgh.

'Have you heard the news?' asked Little Joe.

'Norman's killed himself,' said Danny.

Dusty was already fully informed about this terrible event and explained that in despair after the sudden death of his mother, Norman had thrown himself from a third floor window.

'He was completely dependent on her,' he said.

'Very sad, isn't it?' said Danny. 'Dusty's terribly upset.'

'The funeral was on Monday,' said Dusty. 'They were buried together.'

'I'm full of praise,' intoned the Duke of Edinburgh suddenly. 'What else could he do?'

Months passed. My life changed. In the autumn of that year, I was sacked by the advertising firm and had ideas of becoming a Man of Letters at last. My visits to the West End became irregular. Sometimes I sped past the café in a taxi and was curious to see it crowded and lit up. On other journeys through the West End, I caught glimpses of my former companions. One afternoon I saw one of the waiters bargaining over a piece of flowery fabric in a Soho market, and another day Danny Button surprised me by calling on me in Chelsea.

When I eventually returned to the café, I learned that other changes had taken place. Little Joe now made fewer night-time appearances as the actor he was 'dressing' had taken him under his wing, Dusty informed me, and often dropped him home after work. Passing Little Joe's theatre one night I saw him trotting round a car and getting into the passenger seat.

I asked about the white-haired man with protruding teeth and was told, 'Oh, John only comes in about twice a week now.' One of the waiters, Dusty continued, had taken a job on the telephone exchange and even old Humphrey had not been seen 'for many moons'.

The places vacated by these old favourites were now filled by strangers.

'What salad would you like? Prawn? Ham? Beef? Scotch egg? Cream cheese?' asked Dusty welcoming a new customer and adding, 'I make my best salads in the summer. You need your chicory and your radishes to make up your flavours.'

Later, the stranger asked for 'one of those pink monstrosities on the counter' and found himself slapped into place.

'One of those what?' said Dusty.

'One of those pink things.'

'Oh, strawberry trifle, you mean?'

One evening, a man with pop-out eyes was desperately trying to enjoy himself on the table near the till.

'What time do you close?' he asked, learning the ropes.

'Um – about two,' said Dusty cautiously.

'See you about half-twelve then,' said the newcomer setting off for his evening's work.

New staff were recruited. 'Most of our customers are theatre people – resting, backstage, front-of-house,' I heard Dusty tell one applicant, then, 'Come on Friday. See if you like it. I think you will.'

Miss Fox and the Duke of Edinburgh remained a constant presence and had formed a new alliance. They giggled together like children, laughed at each other's jokes and one evening the old lady particularly amused her companion by asking me rather sharply, 'Getting the proofs next week?'

Another evening, Little Joe surprised me by calling out his telephone number as he left the café. For the next few weeks I made attempts to keep in touch with him. One day I was told he had gone out. 'He's out all day?' I asked. 'He always is, pal.'

I drew another blank the following week – 'He went out ten minutes ago. He won't be back till lateish.' The next time I telephoned, a man with an educated voice told me that Little Joe was there – but in the middle of a card game. He would ring me back.

No call came through and when several months later I tried to contact him again, a voice said, 'I'm afraid Joe left here a long time ago.'

One afternoon I was surprised to find Humphrey back at the café and sitting quietly in a window seat. He had spruced himself up, and was wearing a tight grey suit and a coloured neckerchief. His spectacles were laid out on the table in front of him and his wristwatch, one strap of which was broken, was pinned on to his lapel. He was eating fastidiously – 'I love Dusty's cooking' – and reading an evening newspaper bearing the headline, 'Man Dead in Soho Disturbance'.

'How much do I owe you, Dusty?' he said later, mentioning that he was catching a train to Brighton.

'Humphrey knows the scene,' said Dusty after the old man had shuffled off.

I then made my usual enquiries about Danny and the café's owner whispered that 'the Button' had been under the sun lamp. He had also had some new photographs taken of himself – 'By someone quite good, I believe.'

Suddenly the comedian himself sailed in, on the crest of a wave. He kissed Dusty and sat down beside a young actress. 'I may be going into the Victoria Palace,' he told her presently.

'I'm doing three televisions this month – not in London,' he said a bit later.

'Don't listen to all those lies,' interrupted Dusty without causing offence but making Danny squawk with unusual laughter. Soon he was shouting and thumping his feet on the floor, as if to simulate applause.

'I like it! I like it! I like it!' he screamed after someone had told him a new joke.

Then he came over to my table, complimented me on my new hairstyle – 'Improves you' – and my apparent progress in life. 'You're getting it together,' he told me. 'You started slowly.'

Finally he pressed two of his new photographs upon me. 'Don't just throw them under four hundred of Fred.'

In fact I had not seen Fred for months. His several television appearances had not provided the break he yearned for – and I had lost track of his movements. One day, I telephoned his wife Melody at the old number in Manchester – but even she did not know where he was.

'If you call again next week,' she said crisply, 'I may have some idea.'

The following week, I found the line was out of order.

'Good morning,' I said when I called at the café the following April.

'Good afternoon,' said Dusty, reproving me for my long absence.

The place was empty except for a young man drawing circles round job ads in the early edition of an evening paper. Dusty immediately said he had been 'madly busy all week' and 'every theatre's been packed'.

In many respects the place had changed little during the time I had known it. On the kitchen gramophone, Gertrude Lawrence was singing, 'I'll Follow my Secret Heart' and spread out on the counter were the familiar trays of food.

'Coffee, you said?'

The young proprietor had sprung up from his seat and grabbed at a cup and teaspoon.

'Have you seen Danny Button?' I asked.

'He was in eight times yesterday,' said Dusty, thrusting his head back as he began cutting up salad ingredients.

'Fred phoned Danny on Thursday,' he remarked as his knife sliced into a giant tomato. 'He was in town I suppose.'

Then he tried to persuade me to have something to eat. 'Chocolate gâteau? Florentine? Custard tart? Custard tart is nice.'

April 1966–June 1968

'COULD I SPEAK to Mrs Drinkwater?'

'You are.'

An hour or so later, I stood in front of a huge dark house near the river in Chelsea. It had dozens of blackened windows, many of them curtained or partly blocked by pieces of furniture.

I rang the doorbell and waited for a long time, during which I heard slow dragging footsteps, muffled cries of 'Coming!' and then the unfastening of inner double doors. At last the front door opened and an old woman stood before me, supported on walking-sticks.

'I'm eighty-three years old and in a good deal of pain,' said Mrs Drinkwater as she ushered me into a dark hall, hung with innumerable small family portraits.

A large staircase, covered in an old red carpet, curved grandly upwards but Mrs Drinkwater slowly led the way down a ground-floor passage. Brandishing one stick and leaning on the other, she eventually showed me into a small room at the back of the house.

'It doesn't – ?'

'It doesn't smell. It's shabby but it doesn't smell.'

I took off my camel-hair coat and was left alone. It was a pretty little room, pink-panelled, with a gas ring, a

crucifix above a small bed, two mirrors, a three-cornered
chair upholstered in yellow and a long window overlooking
a garden full of broken furniture and bits of statue half-
submerged in leaves.

For several hours I listened to the footsteps crossing
the uncarpeted room above me, the various creaks and
thuds as Mrs Drinkwater or her other lodgers made their
way about, the crunch of the big front door and the more
remote sound of traffic on Chelsea Embankment.

At first I thought I was entirely alone down my
windowless passage but later that day I heard noises outside
my door. Someone was opening a cupboard, whistling odd
notes as they fiddled about inside it.

Then I heard Mrs Drinkwater's voice far away on an
upper floor.

'Simpson! Simpson! Simpson!'

The person whose head was in the cupboard made no
response other than to murmur a curse. Then my door
opened and an old man in a cap and apron entered the room
carrying two clean sheets. He proceeded to make my bed,
in a very slapdash manner, and left me alone again.

Later, I heard voices in the passage.

'Simpson, before you go, could you see to the lavatory?
It's in an awful mess.'

'Very likely,' said the old man.

For several days and nights I continued to acquaint
myself with the sounds of the house: the thud of footsteps
followed by long periods of silence.

Mrs Drinkwater's life was not an easy one and the
rather elaborate rituals she stuck to did not make it any

easier. Twice a day, creaking floorboards and the clatter of walking-sticks outside my room heralded the opening of the silver cupboard. Then there would be further gasps and groans as my landlady selected her napkin ring.

Shouts for Simpson sometimes alternated with cries of 'Milkman! Milkman!'

Shortly after my arrival I was summoned to the dining-room to pay my rent. Mrs Drinkwater sat neat and tight, underneath a vast portrait of herself as a little girl. A jug of cream remained poised in her hand over a bowl of stewed fruit as she tactfully considered what I owed her.

'I stupidly can't remember what day you came. I think you must have been here a week. If so, you owe me five guineas.'

In spite of her infirmities, Mrs Drinkwater led an active life. I often found her hovering on her own doorstep – an amiable great hedgehog dressed in black from head to foot – waiting to go on some outing. Occasionally, I heard her screaming for a taxi but usually there was a friend coming with a car.

When the vehicle arrived she would make her way to it with difficulty and eventually get in with a sudden jump and cry of triumph. She went out several times a week: to church or some other religious festival, to the opening of an exhibition, to which she had often loaned some artefact, or to tea with some old friend or neighbour.

'She'll kill herself,' said Simpson one morning. 'She stays out late. Stands about in the cold for a taxi. Comes back in pain.'

It was my first conversation with the old man. He told

me that he had worked for Mrs Drinkwater for forty years and since the war had lived with his wife in a council flat behind Chelsea Town Hall.

'With all these motors going about,' he continued, 'it's best to stop at home. We had the chief of police's daughter in last night. Didn't stay long. I'm not much of a one for company.'

One afternoon soon after my arrival, I returned to the house and found an ambulance outside. A very old, thin, tiny little woman was being helped out by two men in uniform. One of them asked, 'Where's your key?'

I followed the procession into the house and found more confusion in the downstairs passage. The old lady was being guided into a small room exactly opposite mine.

'Now then, Miss Fane. All right?' said a burly ambulance man.

'Yes, thank you,' said the old lady meekly.

There were a few minutes of silence after the men had left and then I heard the old lady venturing out along the passage and calling for Mrs Drinkwater.

'Is that you, my dear? Are you there, my dear? Is that you, Bridget?'

Soon the two women were babbling away in the pantry beside the dining-room. Miss Fane was expressing her delight at being back in the house. Mrs Drinkwater was grumbling about Simpson.

'That devil says your accident was all my fault.'

Early the following morning, there was a gentle tapping at my door – I sprang up and opened it.

'Oh, may I come in?' asked Miss Fane.

She looked ill but her tiny features sparkled. She was wearing a faded little suit of black-and-white check and her pointed face was lit up by a scrap of silver curls.

'I'm so delighted,' she said. 'I've found my gold bracelet. I thought I'd left it in the hospital.'

It was the first of many visits, brief conversations. Never a day was to pass without an encounter with this ancient invalid. She visited me to offer pennies for the coin-operated telephone under the stairs and sometimes to ask for little favours in return.

'Oh, could you – would you turn on the tap in the pantry?' she pleaded one afternoon. 'Mrs Drinkwater's turned it off so frightfully hard.'

We talked in the doorway of her own tiny room, from which came a musty smell of Oxo – which she brewed on her gas ring two or three times a day – plus an odour of stale bread and honey and the airlessness caused by keeping the gas fire on all the time. I learned that Miss Fane was in her ninety-third year. She had lived in various flats and houses in different cities – she hankered particularly after the apartment she had given up in Florence at the outbreak of the war. 'It had the most lovely parquet floors.'

She also spoke of her devotion to our landlady – many sentences began, 'Mrs Drinkwater and I' – and she was in awe of her wide-ranging social life. 'Mrs Drinkwater has an enormous circle of friends,' she told me.

I often heard the two women chattering in the pantry.

'Bridget! Bridget!' called Miss Fane in a frail voice. 'Simpson can't be coming.'

'Disgusting of him.'

'I've kept some cheese for you.'

'I can't think what that old fool has done with my biscuits.'

Later that day I heard Mrs Drinkwater saying, 'At least he had the graciousness to send a message of apology.'

Then I heard Miss Fane offering her friend some home-made marmalade. The gift was savagely rejected. 'I can't bear it. I can't bear anything of yours, my dear.'

Soon I heard Simpson clattering about in the pantry again and then the crack of a piece of crockery smashing.

'At least it was before I washed it up,' he muttered.

Then there was puffing and panting and the clicking of walking-sticks as Mrs Drinkwater made her way down the passage to speak to her manservant.

'Now the question is,' she began. 'Half a pint of milk has disappeared. Miss Fane was going to make a sauce.'

Later, Miss Fane came tapping at my door and offered me the rejected jar of marmalade.

'Mrs Drinkwater hates marmalade,' she said with great zest.

Occasionally the conversation between the two women was raised above the domestic level – by Mrs Drinkwater telling Miss Fane about her excursions. One afternoon she had had tea with Sir John Murray at Albemarle Street and been shown the Byron relics – 'Exciting for me, wasn't it?' Another day, she'd attended a gala in honour of the visiting Russian leader.

'I spent the afternoon with the Prime Minister and Mr Kossi-gin. Among a whole lot of other people, of course.'

Mrs Drinkwater's main interest was her own family and she rejoiced when she found anything to do with it at an exhibition.

'Among other things,' she said on her return from a preview at the Victoria and Albert Museum, 'I found a portrait of my great-grandfather and beside the picture was a most interesting, rather long little account of his life.'

But soon the conversation would return to a more humble level.

'Is your kettle boiling by any chance?' Mrs Drinkwater would ask her old lodger. 'It doesn't matter if it's not boiling for me. Thank you so much.'

Day after night, I listened to the sounds of the house. In the morning, I heard the thump-thump-thump of Simpson's progress through the house, his muttered insults and the daily scraping and crashing as he cleaned out the stove in the room above. From far away, on the third or fourth floor, came the long self-important moan of a lodger talking on the telephone – interspersed by strange laughter – and from much closer to hand I heard Miss Fane's frail voice calling 'Bridget! Bridget!' and then the much more commanding tones of Mrs Drinkwater herself, summoning me along to the hall with the words 'William! Telephone!'

One Friday night, well past midnight, I heard slow heavy footsteps in my passage and leapt from my bed to lock the door.

The same footsteps were repeated the next day and I heard a loud female voice asking, 'Are you there, Miss Fane?'

There was no reply from the old lady's room – but I soon heard the sound of her door being opened and the visitor sniffing.

Then there was another footstep and an aggressive

knock on my own door. A ring on the stranger's finger hit the wood.

I opened the door to a dowdy, middle-aged woman carrying a bottle of wine. She told me she had just been superannuated from her job. She lived in a room at the top of the house and had no money to pay her rent.

'I'm not sorry,' she shouted. 'Think of Christ going barefoot. The Son of God was hungry. Are you a Catholic?'

'Are you?'

'No – I have my own church. The Church of God. I'm not going until you pour yourself a glass of wine. I thought you were a Catholic. How much do you pay for this room? Ten guineas, I'd guess. I pay eighty-five shillings. I'm only a second-class citizen. What do you do?'

Eventually she moved to go. At the door she turned back.

'I'm not sorry, you see. I shall buy a frying pan and cook myself a chop.'

There were at least ten other lodgers – 'PGs' Mrs Drinkwater called them – a floating population in various states of poverty, eccentricity and foreignness. Mrs Drinkwater obtained them through friends of friends and communicated with them partly by leaving messages on the large hall table.

'Miss Burton. Can you let me have some cash tonight as I am very short.'

'Mr Waddilove. I don't think you have paid for the week of thirtieth May to June fifth.'

Other messages were addressed to the whole household.

'This key was found in the door between eight and nine last night. Not a good plan.'

'I spend large sums of money having the bathrooms repainted and then someone splashes on dashes of red paint.'

'Front door open again. Midnight Tuesday.'

A few of the lodgers also used the hall table to make general announcements.

'To Whom It May Concern', an aggressive hand had scribbled. 'Will you please leave my newspaper in peace in the morning.' This angry note was signed 'Waddilove'.

It was at the hall table that I met other lodgers each morning.

One woman with a cigarette in her mouth would spend several minutes there, dropping ash on to the incoming letters and newspapers. 'Expecting something important?' she asked when I hesitated beside her. 'Well, not really important,' I replied.

Another morning, after I had sorted the post myself, I was upbraided by the lodger named Waddilove. 'Did you put the letters out?' 'I may have missed some of them.' 'I should say so.'

Several of the lodgers did not work – or even get properly dressed. One day I found a huge bald-headed woman in a red dressing-gown waiting around for her books to arrive from Harrods Lending Library. 'Good mornin', darlin',' she said in a surprisingly leisurely voice. Then a young foreigner in a black cloak rushed past and out into the street shouting, 'Is there a taxi there?'

One day, Mrs Drinkwater talked about her lodgers. 'That tiresome Russian woman whom Simpson dislikes. I don't care for her much myself . . . Mr Waddilove's had one operetta produced, that's all. And he's very lucky to have had that ... I did Mr Browning a good turn having him here and now he's invited a whole lot of tiresome people ... Miss de Winter is an invalid. She's not been out of this house twelve years ... Miss Burton is a very hard-working woman ... My young Argentinian PG hates everyone, including himself. I dare say there's something nice underneath but I can't get through to it.'

She also talked about Miss Fane and prayed that she was not being a nuisance to me.

'She's a lady but, oh, what a bore she can be,' she said tersely. 'And of course the thing is she can't read since her accident.'

'Her accident?'

'It happened during a blackout in March. I had a torch beside me – but she got nervous and started walking along to the dining-room. Then she decided that she was being stupid and started going back. Of course you can't judge the distance in the dark and the poor thing thought she was back at her own door when in fact she was at the top of the cellar steps! By the time I got here, all I could hear was moaning. I started climbing down the steps and found I was wading through pools of blood. She was lying at the bottom in another pool of blood, wailing "My arm! My leg! My head!" Amazingly, nothing was broken. She went to hospital for ten days and, of course, they let her out far, far too soon.'

Miss Fane seemed to have recovered from the mishap and even managed to get some daily exercise. I often heard her tip-tapping along the uncarpeted passage and then the slam of the front door as she went out. One afternoon she told me she had had lunch in a new King's Road café called Guys and Dolls.

'I had some rav-i-ol-i,' she said, relishing every syllable.

Summer came. Simpson sported a jaunty yellow Tootal tie – 'I've got a drawerful like this at home.' Miss Fane appeared in an old butterfly-encrusted hat. Each night, I returned exhausted, peeled off my clothes and opened the window on to the garden.

At the end of July, Mrs Drinkwater went off by long-distance coach to stay with cousins in the West Country.

In her absence, the household became more chaotic. One day I heard the Russian lodger calling out in the street that she had lost her key. On another occasion I found the superannuated lodger drifting out of Mrs Drinkwater's private quarters.

One night I had to carry a message to the top of the house. It was a strange little community up there. A radio played and there was a stink of cigarettes – many of the lodgers were chain-smokers. Someone was listening to *The Archers* and in a room shared by two girls, a fierce argument was taking place.

'You are a bloody liar.'

'I am not a bloody liar.'

It was during Mrs Drinkwater's holiday that another near-disaster befell Miss Fane. One night as she was preparing for bed, a large brick hurtled through her window. It crashed on to a table, smashing the top of an empty Gentleman's Relish jar – provided as an ashtray – and landed at the old lady's feet.

'Oh, may I come and see you?' she asked excitedly after the incident but not apparently in the least alarmed by it.

The following day, Simpson patched up the hole with part of an old suitcase and some string.

'Oh, my dear,' said Mrs Drinkwater on her return. 'I never heard anything so awful as your window.'

Miss Fane was determined to make light of the affair and seemed far more concerned about an uncovered workman's hole in the street outside the house.

'Simpson might fall into it and break his neck,' she said.

My room had its own bathroom attached to it in which there was no lavatory. I was obliged to use the one in the hall. From here I would hear other lodgers talking on the coin-operated telephone under the stairs.

'Did you get home all right?' a girl asked one night. 'You got the bus all right? I'll give you a ring later, Mummy.'

Then I heard the aggressive voice of the musical Mr Waddilove accepting an invitation.

'Yes, yes, it would be very nice. Yes, yes, lovely. But, er, will you be sure to have food? Otherwise – um—'

Other conversations involving Waddilove ended more abruptly – 'Well, that's a good answer. Goodbye!' – and sometimes the telephone was rudely slammed down.

Often the telephone was picked up by one person, and another person would be summoned from several floors above. One afternoon the big stairwell reverberated with cries of, 'Antoine! Telephone!'

'For me?' came a feeble voice three floors above.

'He is coming,' said the man who had first picked up the telephone.

Then came a flurry of descending footsteps and the breathless words, 'Hello, yes, Antoine speaking. Oh, I am so sorry. We shall postpone the evening? You have consulted a doctor?'

Mrs Drinkwater only used this telephone when her own one was out of order or when she could not face the climb to her first-floor drawing-room.

'Is that Mary-Josephine? It's Bridget. Very lame, I'm afraid. John Gay dined here last night and told me you were in London. Mmmm? Yes. Do!'

Another time I heard her talking to the grocery store at the corner of the street.

'Would you believe it? My telephone's out of order again. The day before yesterday, nobody could get through at all. I'll have two peaches and a packet of Ryvita.'

It was after this particular conversation that Mrs Drinkwater began advancing towards the lavatory in which I sat listening. When she eventually reached the door, she rattled and wrenched at the handle for several moments before realizing that the room was occupied.

Though frugal and self-denying, Mrs Drinkwater was extremely hospitable and often had friends in for tea and at other times of the day.

When her visitors rang the doorbell, there was always frantic shuffling and the familiar cries of 'Coming! Coming!'

Usually I did not see the guests but I heard their voices from my room and saw their discarded outer clothing in the hall. One afternoon there was a black Homburg on the hall table. Late one autumn night there were two or three dark coats slung over the stair rail with opera programmes sticking out of their pockets.

Guests varied. Once I saw a nun in the hall. One afternoon's caller was an eminent elderly politician who had just published his memoirs. Amidst the clatter of walking-sticks, I heard this visitor and Mrs Drinkwater greeting each other.

'Nice to see you . . .'

'Indeed I do . . .'

'I'm very lame. I'll just fetch the kettle off the stove. Let's turn on a light.'

'Can I help you?'

'I've done it now. Well, I enjoyed that book enormously. I saw it was on Harrods' list of good books.'

Sooner or later, the dining-room door would close and the voices became muffled. Sometimes, if drinking was taking place, the voices would become louder again and one particular speaker might seem to be shouting his head off.

Eventually, the guests would emerge, don their hats and coats – 'You can see me now in my Moscow regalia' – and utter further pleasantries as they made their departures.

Once she had bid her guests 'Goodnight', Mrs Drink-water would close the front door rather noisily and have a fit of coughing.

Miss Fane played little part in these entertainments. When Mrs Drinkwater was alone the two women had their simple meals together in a dark corner of the dining-room, but more festive events usually took place without the older lady.

'I had a nice visit from my Mary-Josephine,' Mrs Drinkwater might say later. Or, 'I was talking to Miss Broakes most amiably.'

Miss Fane did not go to bed early. I often heard her groping around her room after midnight. When she eventually retired, these noises did not cease and I would sometimes return to the house after a long evening in the West End and hear her talking quite loudly in her sleep, her ancient voice forming indistinguishable words.

Each morning, she would be up long before me. I was sometimes woken by the sound of a discussion between her and Simpson. The old man arrived each morning at seven, his first duty being to prepare Mrs Drinkwater's scrambled egg – a task which she said he did better than anyone she had ever known.

Winter came. The wind blew down my chimney and stretched the wooden panels of the door. Simpson was good enough to see that I needed another blanket. Through the leafless branches of the tree outside my window I could see into the house opposite. Two women were standing in a room, one of them dangling something in her hand.

One December morning I stooped and lit the old gas fire and then sat watching the small blue flames rising and falling inside the antique filaments. Later Miss Fane appeared in a fur helmet and coat.

'I'm like Peary going to the North Pole,' she said.

Another day an announcement from Mrs Drinkwater appeared on the hall table.

'The front and inner doors were wide open at 10.45 last night. Cold and dangerous.'

It was followed by a more modest message.

'If anyone is going out, will they please post this letter?'

The winter did not worry Simpson. Even on a day when there was snow on the ground he arrived wearing a yellow scarf but no socks. He then changed into battered woollen slippers, remarking, 'Any old shoes do for dodging about the house.'

'Isn't he droll?' said Miss Fane.

At Christmas, Mrs Drinkwater set up a huge illuminated crib in the hall, with twenty or thirty shepherds, animals and other supporting figures arranged around it.

Early in the New Year, I got a job in advertising – 'That racket!' guffawed Simpson – but the house remained my home and I continued to follow the fortunes of its inmates. One weekend, I heard squabbling in Miss Fane's bedroom.

'You mustn't go out until the congestion and inflammation has gorn,' said Mrs Drinkwater.

'You can't expect a thing like that to go,' argued Miss Fane bravely.

'No, indeed not.'

At first, Miss Fane stubbornly ignored her friend's protestations and tried to change the subject – 'I heard the word grapefruit mentioned' – but after a crescendo of further protests, she caved in completely.

'I feel weak. So frightfully weak.'

A doctor was summoned but took his time coming. Much later that day Miss Fane tapped on my door and said, 'Dr Higgs still hasn't come. What's going to happen to me now?'

Loud footsteps of the doctor came down the passage

the following morning and were followed by his gentle
words to the old lady.

'Could I just have a look at you? That'll do, yes.'

Then he said, 'I wonder if you'd take one of these
tablets every morning?' and closed his case with a thump
and a click.

Miss Fane soon reappeared at my door, looking quite
desperately ill, one eye quite soggy with blood.

'The doctor says I mayn't go out,' she said in the voice
of a scolded child.

In spite of her illness she refused to have a hot-water
bottle.

'You must!' ordered Mrs Drinkwater. 'If you don't
have one, I shall scream.'

On this issue too, Miss Fane eventually caved in.

'Goodnight, dear. Thank you,' she said finally, in a
slurred voice.

The old lady's health did not improve – 'I don't think
I'm much better', 'No, indeed not' – and a few days later it
was decided that she should return to hospital. The two
friends were now bickering about arrangements. Miss Fane
wanted to take her fur coat. Mrs Drinkwater warned her
that this might not be possible.

'They were very tiresome about Aunty Betty's clothes,'
she said. 'They were very tiresome about my clothes. They
wrap you up very warmly, you know.'

Miss Fane also implored Mrs Drinkwater to visit her
as often as possible.

'I'll do my best to come this week. I know I can't
come on Thursday. I'll do my best to come on Friday and
Sunday.'

I woke up on the morning of Miss Fane's departure to find her bedroom light on and hear her scuffling about in the passage. Then came further discussions about milk: 'This new pint that Simpson has gone and got.'

The weekend after Miss Fane's admission to hospital there was a heavy downfall of rain. All the old gutters and drainpipes of the house were immediately in service. Obliged to go out in a hurry, I recklessly snatched up an umbrella in the hall.

Two days later, unfamiliar footsteps came down my passage and my door flew open.

'Have you got my umbrella?' demanded Mr Waddilove.

'No, I'm sorry, I did take it at the weekend but I returned it,' I mumbled.

'Well, it's gone again. You are the only other man in the house at the moment. Have you lost it?'

'No, I only took it for a few minutes and I returned it,' I repeated.

'I don't believe you.'

Later when I heard Mrs Drinkwater locking up the silver cupboard outside my room, I seized the chance to tell her of the umbrella's second disappearance.

'I'm afraid Mr Waddilove thinks I've taken it again and lost it,' I explained.

'Well, I've told him firmly you haven't,' she said.

Later I heard her addressing the composer on the staircase.

'Only a bore like you would dare to be rude to me!' she shouted.

A week or so later, I visited Miss Fane in the Brompton Hospital. A nurse directed me vaguely to one side of the large public ward where dozens of silent shrivelled women lay on high beds.

Eventually I found my fellow lodger. She lay like a bird with a broken wing, half-asleep, her tiny head on a huge white pillow. A claw of a hand, with an ugly identification disc round the wrist, half-buried her face. I touched her elbow.

She flickered into consciousness, opened her eyes and recognized me. In a weak voice, she told me she hated leaving Chelsea and was looking forward so much to getting back to her own room.

'All my friends, all the shops I know, are in Chelsea.'

Walking back from the hospital, I ran into the angry Mr Waddilove in King's Road. He gave me a thin smile.

'The umbrella has been returned. Broken.'

Back at the house I heard the sound of a brush and pan being used in Miss Fane's room and found Simpson on his hands and knees. The room had been cleared out and the patched-up window was left wide open. In the hall, I heard Mrs Drinkwater talking to a middle-aged woman who appeared to be Miss Fane's niece.

'We had to charge her for gas,' said Mrs Drinkwater. 'She uses such a lot.'

'I know she does,' said the stranger.

Hanging on the bottom stair rail was Miss Fane's black-and-white check suit, back from the dry-cleaner's with sixteen shillings and sixpence to pay.

A few days later, the small room opposite was

repainted and available again – a black man was among those who came to look at it – and Mrs Drinkwater embarked upon a more extensive programme of spring-cleaning.

She did much of the work herself, donning a pink overall and also getting down on her hands and knees.

'I've been doing tidying jobs in my bedroom,' she explained to a visitor. 'It means taking down all the pictures and cleaning them.'

She also discussed this time-honoured procedure with Simpson. 'We could have done this much more easily in the drawing-room,' she said – and then, 'What is the alternative? A hell of a bore!' and 'Well, that was the idea.'

At other times the old man evaded and enraged her and I heard her shrieking his name until she was breathless.

'Is that you, Simpson?' she said at last. 'There are no tea-cloths in the pantry.'

My own encounters with my landlady remained harmonious. Sometimes suddenly face to face, teapot in hand, she said simply, 'Ah!' but often she was remarkably chatty and even apologetic. 'I do hope the passage is not fearfully wet for you,' she said during the spring-cleaning operation.

'I'm so worried about Simpson being a nuisance,' she said more than once but she still seemed in awe of the old man. 'Simpson was very cross with me,' she said one morning after staying out later than usual and receiving the lash of his tongue.

Miss Fane left hospital but she did not return to the house.

'She became quite seriously ill,' said Mrs Drinkwater in answer to another lodger's enquiries. The lives of the two

women were still entwined however and it appeared that
Mrs Drinkwater was now trying to get a place for her old
lodger in a local convent.

Letters and postcards from Miss Fane to Mrs Drinkwater began to appear on the hall table.

On a picture postcard of The Iron Bridge, Newport
Pagnell, Miss Fane had written, 'I miss you very much. I
am getting a little better and I think the air is doing me
good. Please see if the convent beds are as comfortable and
long as yours – and sprung mattresses. When my money
comes from France, please send me £4.'

A more urgent request for money followed a few days
later on a plain postcard.

'My niece said it was for me to buy myself luxuries. I
have been here two weeks and need the money. I've sent
the stamp for postage.'

A few weeks later, I returned from work to find Mrs
Drinkwater answering a further enquiry from a lodger
about Miss Fane.

'Yes, she died last night in the convent,' she said.

'You can't beat living,' said Simpson. 'I had chicken, carrots
and turnips for lunch. The only trouble is my lumbago.
Every time you try to pick something up you think you're
going to fall over.'

'Nice cap,' I said.

'Got to look as smart as you can.'

The old man's relationship with his employer
remained volatile and his mischief reached new heights.

'I haven't seen you for a long time,' he said to her one
day in the pantry. 'Where have you been hiding?'

Sometimes I heard them talking together very gently. 'What a good idea, yes, do!' Mrs Drinkwater was saying. Then came angry tones – 'All right, all right, I'll go,' and the muttered words, 'Old bag!'

Another morning, I heard Mrs Drinkwater shouting, 'You say I should get up earlier. I probably should. But why mention doctors? It's an aggravating habit of yours.'

'I'm very wicked,' replied the old man.

'You're not wicked,' screamed Mrs Drinkwater. 'You're just terribly, terribly rude.'

'Oh dear. Such a pity,' declared Mrs Drinkwater when almost a year later I said I had some rather tiresome news for her.

'Too dirty?' she asked immediately and then later in the day, 'I'm so sad you're going.'

'Yes, it's very sad.'

Simpson took the news more coolly and when I explained that I was moving into a building down the street, said, 'I used to work there. Well, never mind. Got a nice flat?'

A few days later, Mrs Drinkwater left a note for me on the hall table.

'Do you know when you want to go? Because I have an offer for your room. I would like you to stay.'

Simpson tried another angle.

'What are you going to give me when you leave? A fiver?'

On my last morning in the house, I heard the old man counting plates in the pantry. He spoke to himself in a loud clear voice.

'One, two, three, four, five, six . . .'

January 1967–October 1968

GORDON WAS SMALL and portly and wore a tight-fitting waistcoat. Out of the back pocket of his trousers protruded an enormous comb, which he ran through his glossy black hair within moments of entering the room. He then approached my desk rather gingerly.

'Yes, I heard you were joining us today,' he began in a cordial voice.

Suddenly, the door flew open and another man sailed in. He was pale but eager-looking. He wore a short blue reefer jacket and a scarf which he took off and threw over the pegs by the door.

'Sorry I'm late. I got some cotton wool stuck in my nose and had to pop along to the doctor.'

The newcomer greeted me, introduced himself as Toby, and went off to get coffee for us both. As we drank this, he began to quiz me about myself in a leisurely and friendly manner. Soon he had lit a cigarette and put his feet up, not just on his desk but on his typewriter. Meanwhile, Gordon had slid back comfortably into his corner seat and was beginning to glance through the messages and memos on his desk.

'Stupid buggers,' he muttered.

The fourth desk in the room was soon occupied by a

soft-featured girl whose shaggy blonde hair was hidden on
arrival by a big fur hat, which she carefully took off and
placed on a shelf. Her name was Sue. At first I thought she
must be a typist or secretary.

'I'm sorry. What is your name?' she asked.

Toby then told Sue that he had had a dream about her
hat. She smiled politely as she went off to the ladies'
cloakroom and Toby continued his friendly inquisition
about my past.

'You must have had a hell of a lot of laughs,' he said.

In return, he then revealed that he had spent most of
the previous year in France writing a novel and had only
taken this job to keep him going while he looked for
something better. He was divorced, living in a rented flat
in Islington. He had a girlfriend but would also, he said,
like to seduce Sue.

Gordon soon interrupted these disclosures by asking
in an amiable voice, 'Could I have a word with you, Toby,
in about five minutes?'

He then turned to the girl who I now realized was also
a copywriter.

'Sue, how are you fixed?'

Gordon then outlined various pieces of work and
asked, 'Okay?'

'Yeh . . .'

'Knock-out!' exclaimed Gordon, crumpling a sheet of
paper into a ball and throwing it across the room into the
bin beside my desk.

Later in the morning a large lopsided man in a high-
collared green suit and big spectacles entered the room to
see Gordon. I recognized Raikes, who had interviewed me

for the job. He greeted me enthusiastically – 'You look super' – but had difficulty remembering my name. 'Is it William?' he asked, eyes rolling.

Thus began my first morning in one of London's biggest advertising agencies. The firm employed over three hundred people and handled a wide variety of accounts, including famous consumer goods, services and industrial products. The eighty or so of us on the fourth floor – the building was a minor West End landmark – were divided into groups of writers and designers. Soon after my arrival, Sue explained to me that ours was one of the 'star' groups.

'Gordon has carved out an image for himself and his work. He sells himself and his work. His gloss rubs off on the group.'

'Half your work will be TV,' Raikes had told me at the interview but Gordon seemed in no hurry to start me on any particular task.

Instead, I listened to the hum of activity all around us. The offices were thinly partitioned from one another and you could hear a continual murmur of telephones, the clack of typewriters and crescendos of conversation, often interspersed with squeaks and screams of laughter, even snatches of song. Cries of 'Oooh! Subtle!' and 'Oh! No! Stop! Horrible!' were followed by words from 'Ha-Ha Said The Clown' or some other contemporary hit.

All day long people entered our office. One of my first visitors was a small woman in a cardigan. She approached my desk, stated my name and departed without a flicker of a smile. Later, a taller, more commanding lady swept into the room and began rummaging behind me for a missing file. From her painted lips came the name of a well-known washing-up liquid, repeated over and over as the search extended to my desk.

Every so often, the door opened and an elderly messenger appeared with a post-bag in his arms. One of these men was half-paralysed and I watched with concern as he groped at the In and Out trays near the doorway. His colleague suffered from poor sight and needed to take off his spectacles as he slowly sorted our correspondence.

The most insistent visitors were the account executives from the floor below. They came to chase up our work, congratulate us, break the news that everything had been rejected or seek out one of us in particular.

'Where is Gordon?' said a man in a silver tie. 'He promised me faithfully he'd be here at half-past three.'

''Ello dere,' said a more scruffy figure imitating a negro and then adding, 'Hi, Toby, how are things?'

'*Comment ça va?*' another caller asked later – and Toby responded to these pleasantries with civilities of his own. 'Is that an order, sir?' he meekly enquired.

'Bloody nice ads, Sue,' said another young executive who swivelled his body like a bronco billy and ended his visit with the words, 'You're doing a grand job, Sue. Bysie!'

Sometimes more magisterial figures leant through the door with more solemn requests.

'A word with you, Gordon, if you can spare a moment,' said such a person one morning – and Gordon trotted off immediately to this man's office.

I soon realized that there was a constant battle being waged between the so-called 'creative' people and these executives – but Gordon was usually able to cope with the challenge.

'That wildly efficient account executive makes me feel slightly agitated,' he admitted after one encounter but he was soon fuming, 'Ridiculous bloody people. Who handles this account? I'm not going to have my group's work mucked up. If necessary, I go to Jack Beastly.'

An angry telephone call followed, which ended with Gordon saying, 'With the proviso that they don't offload their muck on to me.'

Even Sue was capable of asserting herself, cornering an opponent on the phone. 'Tim – it's Sue. Could I make a strong personal plea about something?' After further forceful words, she added, 'Let's just say I'm keeping my end up.'

Among other visitors to our offices were the designers and typographers from across the corridor. These unassuming figures, some in home-knitted sweaters, worked all day in an airless room with Cow Gum and other substances. They had far more professional qualifications than the writers but were more modest and industrious by nature. 'I'll get back and do some work,' remarked one of them on finding Gordon occupied on the telephone.

Twice a day the rattle of wheels, often audible in the distance, suddenly got much louder. Tea or coffee had arrived. The lady responsible first took the briefest possible peek through the door to see who was present and then dispensed tea or coffee from a trolley in the corridor. Four lumps of sugar were provided with each cup, and sometimes a biscuit. More senior personnel were given a cup and saucer with a gold rim, for which there was a special compartment on the vehicle.

The ladies who performed these rituals were sardonic and unpredictable. When I bade one of them 'Good morning,' she twisted round like a wounded animal. When I asked, 'What's the biscuit situation?' the same lady said chirpily, 'Lousy at the moment.'

Though the drinks themselves were disgusting – the coffee tasted as if the juice of a poisonous plant had been squeezed into it – Toby always tried to get more than his one cup, often seeking out the little pantry where the drinks were prepared or sending me to do it for him.

One morning, I found the coffee lady kneeling on the floor picking up fragments of a broken cup.

'At least it was before I washed it up,' she said.

I passed on Toby's request but she refused to oblige him. 'Tell him he's already had two cups. He had one with Fothergill.'

Fothergill was one of the most frequent visitors to our office. He was the firm's creative director. A small, energetic ex-army officer, he had run the firm's creative department for the last ten years. He had a schoolmaster's or, more accurately, school chaplain's face, small gold spectacles, loops of red flesh, slicked-back hair, rigid clean white teeth and a permanent rash of spots over part of his face and neck. His little blue suits, trousers caked in gloss, red spotted ties and handkerchiefs, expensive frayed shirts and old suede shoes gave the impression that he led the life of leisure outside the office. On site, he was efficent and fast-moving. Sometimes his mask-like face appeared at the door of our office, saw that Gordon was absent and vanished without saying a word. Fothergill and I were never properly introduced. Often he stood at the door chattering to my colleagues but ignoring me. 'Complete crap,' he barked one afternoon. 'I mean, God almighty, what's happened to our common sense?'

'Well, quite,' said Gordon.

'Brainstorms are a bloody waste of time. I mean the way you get ads is by sitting down and thinking of them.'

'Those are my sentiments exactly,' said Gordon.

'I suppose Sue hasn't got any spare time?' said Fothergill.

''Fraid not.'

'I imagine she hasn't, no.'

The creative director's attention then turned briefly to a new product on which the group would soon start working.

'I think we should call in John Coventry.'

'What for?' asked Gordon.

'Bits and pieces. I predict lots of bits and pieces.'

Finally Fothergill left the room, asking in a singsong voice, 'When shall we three meet again? In thunder, lightning or rain?' Shifting his energetic little body through the doorway he suddenly cast an expressionless glance in my direction.

'What a thing it is to be solemn,' he said.

In spite of this bleakness between us, I was constantly aware of the creative director's presence and pronouncements. I heard his God Almightys and Complete Craps in the corridor and often passed the open door of his office where he sat comfortably talking into a dictaphone or making private telephone calls of his own. 'Good afternoon,' I heard him say one lunch-time. 'Could I talk to Mr Jack Hawkins?'

The deputy creative director, Raikes, was a more slippery figure. He often seemed to be putting on his overcoat and going off to see clients. I had seen him crossing the road in heavy rain. I had met his big, ugly spectacles and sideburns in the lavatory and the lift, where he stood impatiently shaking the loose change in his trouser pocket. I had also noticed that his responses to me were now much cooler. 'Hello, er, William,' was all he would manage.

When he appeared in our office it was often to try and enlist Gordon's support for some new scheme to oust Fothergill.

Most of our time in the office was spent chatting – or teasing each other. When Sue announced that she had a cold, Toby said immediately, 'Take lots of champagne and a man to bed.' When Toby embraced Gordon after a successful client presentation, Gordon responded, 'Get off me, you raving homosexual!'

Even the executives who visited us were often on a purely social call. They sat on our desks and engaged us in conversation. One man mentioned playing darts. 'There's something lovely about standing there floating them into a board. You sit on your arse all day.' Another talked about a house he had found in Fulham. 'In a dinky little street. Just like a doll's house. With a four-poster bed.'

'It must be tricky looking for a house on foot,' remarked Gordon.

These visitors came in all shapes and styles. One man

wore a cloak, another thick crêpe rubber shoes. Some chewed gum, several wiggled their bottoms. If they had no news from the outside world, they cast an eye over the papers on our desks.

'Oh, my God!' exclaimed an executive one morning. 'Gordon's finished his crossword!'

Another day, a man with a bright orange pigskin briefcase called with a more specific purpose.

'Gordon,' he began. 'Do you – would you like to play football? I'm sketching out a team – the team – to play Cadbury's. I pictured you as a left-winger. Lots of clever side steps.'

'What's this?' said Toby suddenly waking up. 'I'd love to play.'

Another time, an executive arrived with a big box of potato crisps – one of the products we worked on. Gordon slashed it open with his comb and distributed a few packets. At the end of the day, a typist from the end of the corridor went off with the remainder.

When we were alone, the various power structures within the firm were discussed and the reputations of colleagues torn to shreds.

'This politicking is extraordinary,' said Gordon one morning after a visit from the deputy creative director. 'Raikes does it more than anyone I know. Fothergill doesn't do it.'

'I smell dirty business,' said Toby. 'What Raikes is doing is, quite obviously, stalling.'

'Of course he's trying to displace Fothergill,' said Gordon.

'Which I think is a dirty one.'

'Oh, I think Fothers can look after himself.'

'Raikes is clever,' insisted Toby. 'In the most evil and scheming way.'

Toby had his own grievance to air. 'For Christ's sake, don't tell anyone, but when I joined here four months ago, Raikes promised to make me a group head. We worked together at Boxleys.'

Although on the whole Toby and Gordon seemed to favour the ex-officer rather than his upstart deputy, Fothergill also came in for criticism.

'Fothergill's ideas are very ordinary but he's superb at selling them,' said Gordon.

The two men had decided that the creative director was basically very shy, made bitchy remarks and had a strong feminine streak. By the end of this particular discussion, Gordon and Toby had decided that Fothergill was, in fact, very likely, queer.

As soon as Gordon was out of the room, Toby talked equally frankly about him too. 'Gordon is a little, little man,' he said. 'He doesn't stop at stealing other people's ideas either.' His main contempt was reserved for Sue. Until quite recently he had wanted to seduce Sue. Now he was sick of her.

'She has no heights, no depths,' he suddenly stormed. 'Sue is nothing. No sex, no events, no problems – she's nothing. Why's she so conventional? Those kooky hats and mini-skirts! Why can't she let her hair down?'

Toby also said that he despised Sue's work.

'Sue simply imitates the best advertisements.'

To her face, Toby remained as obsequious, or flirtatious, as ever. 'Much less bother,' he explained to me after congratulating her on 'a lovely bit of copy'.

Alone with me, Toby was as warm and friendly as he was to everyone else. When I expressed doubts about my survival in the firm, he assured me, 'You haven't got a cat's chance in hell of being sacked,' and he flattered me further by adding, 'You are the only person here I could possibly ask to a party.'

From time to time, Gordon and Toby talked about other agencies – 'Boxleys have chopped a lot of people recently' – and made unfavourable comparisons with our own firm.

'Of course, this place has its advantages,' said Toby.

'Oh, for Christ's sake, yes,' said Gordon.

Sometimes a deeper note was struck and these conversations took a philosophical turn. Literature was touched upon – 'To be honest,' said Toby, 'I think Jane Austen's a frantic old bore' – and also religion. 'Once you've sorted out religion, you can get on with the rest of life,' said Gordon.

Sometimes Gordon and Toby talked about themselves. Toby confessed that he was 'slightly paranoiac' and one morning revealed that he had burst into tears while watching a television film. Then he talked about 'the snake pit of self-doubt' and insecurity in general.

'As soon as you begin to let it get you down, you're in trouble,' he said facing his typewriter, his voice dying out.

Gordon talked cheerily about 'the *route nationale*', 'the Italian art cities' and 'fat little Frenchmen with napkins under their chins' but disclosed that his real ambition was to live in a cottage somewhere in England with a 'woman' and his five friends around him. He claimed that he had long ago cut himself off from his family after a series of quarrels during his late teens.

'In actual fact,' he said, 'one's parents have no right at all to interfere with one's life.'

Further revelations included the fact that Gordon, too, had recently finished a novel – 'When this one's out of the way, I'll probably start another' – and ended with a plea from Toby for confidentiality. 'I've only told you all this because you're a friend,' he said.

'Sure,' replied Gordon.

Gordon was frequently on the telephone chatting with one or other of his Five Friends and arranging to meet them.

'Yes, indeed. How about lunch? How are you fixed for eating there? No, I don't like Indian food. What I like is a steak. Shall I come over to you or shall we meet halfway?'

'What's been happening?' he asked another friend. 'What's been going on? Are you still going out with Mandy? Great! Well, how about dinner, sort of this week? Today, any day except Thursday. I don't go out much in the winter. Tonight? Okay, I'll tell Jill.'

Sue's ball-point pen twiddled in her hand as Gordon rang through to the girl he lived with.

'Andy and bird will be presenting themselves at about eight. I thought we'd eat in probably. Bye, sweetheart.'

Another afternoon, one of these Five Friends called in person on Gordon and was subjected to questioning about his career – or lack of one.

'I'm doing lots of other things too,' said the visitor.

'Great,' said Gordon. 'What sort of things?'

The real love of Gordon's life was his sports car and this was also the subject of many telephone calls. When speaking to his garage, he faced the window and used a low voice.

'Mr Gummer please. Thank you. Hello, did you get my note? How is everything? The thing is it's tending to jump forward as it rolls to a halt.'

A further call to a friend who shared this particular interest ended with the question, 'What about Brand's Hatch? The track's open till the end of the month.'

Toby's telephone calls tended to be of a more sombre nature and were accompanied by clouds of cigarette smoke. One day, about five weeks after my arrival in the firm, his landlord rang to say that his rent cheque had bounced. Toby replaced the receiver slowly, sat motionless for a moment and then began to imitate the noise of a bomb exploding. I noticed that the flex of his telephone was badly tangled and there were loose cigarettes all over the desk.

'How are you, William?' he suddenly asked brightly.

Within minutes, Toby had put the bounced cheque to the back of his mind and was involved in some repartee with a visiting executive, laughing and scratching his cheek at the same time.

Another of Toby's problems was his mother. Smoke billowed out of his nose one afternoon as he waited on the telephone to speak to a sister-in-law.

'What I'm going to say is nothing because I'm afraid it's going to have to be a surprise. How long will it take before the creditors are paid? If Samuels ring that's what we've got to tell them. When Bill rang last night he was bringing up all sorts of problems I thought I'd settled with Rosie.'

There was also a problem over the custody of a child – but all these challenges he met bravely and without self-pity. Sometimes he even seemed to enjoy the fight.

'I'm arranging my mother's affairs, and putting them under a court of protection,' he told Gordon.

A few days later, things had taken a turn for the better and his mother had been installed in hospital. Toby strode round the office with his trousers sagging at his ankles. He looked as if he had just won a gladiatorial contest. He was himself again, chuckling down the telephone when an old friend rang up. 'I laughed like a drain when I got your reply! Great man!'

Replacing the telephone, he clapped his hands and then rubbed them together. After fumbling among his papers, he suddenly thrust a copy of the *Daily Express* into Gordon's hands. The newspaper had been folded to empha-size the photograph of a model girl.

'Who's this?' asked Gordon rather impatiently.

'My girlfriend,' said Toby.

'Oh, super.'

Later, Toby offered Gordon a chocolate but our boss was now talking on the telephone and pushed it away saying nothing. The two men's desks reflected their differ-ent characters. Gordon's desk was neat and clean. Discreet against the wall was a box from Austin Reed's with a new white towel dressing-gown in it – 'Gordon likes to buy a lot of things,' Sue had told me. Toby's desk was getting more and more muddled. A bundle of solicitor's letters nudged against a heavy pottery ashtray laden with cigarette ends smoked to the hilt. Toby's old tin lighter rolled around under his papers. Gordon's ritzy one was always standing on its end and he carried his smart steel ashtray with him when he crossed the room. Both men were overweight, but Toby's tummy fell out of his shirt in a sloppy manner while Gordon's was held in by his trendy suit. Toby's ties were old-fashioned, thin and faded – and tied in an untidy manner. Gordon's were brand new and very wide, pinned on to his chest like napkins and worn with floppy-collared shirts.

Toby was outspoken and clumsy. Gordon was suave and diplomatic.

'It's a point of view,' he said when Toby had criticized a new commercial. 'Not one on which I'd take issue.'

Finishing his chocolates and facing his typewriter again, Toby could not concentrate. There was a long silence. Then suddenly he decided he had a headache.

'I think I'll blow off for a bit and lie down.'

One spring morning, the creative director Fothergill stood just inside our office, fiddling with a new sheepskin jacket that Gordon had just bought and which now hung on a peg beside my camel-hair coat.

'Very handsome that. A bit warm for today, I should think.'

Gordon did not look up from his desk.

Fothergill turned his attention to Sue, walked over to her desk and asked jokily, 'Is Sue in this morning?' and then added in his singsong voice, 'Oh, dear, what can the matter be?'

Suddenly Toby came swinging in with a cup of coffee, almost colliding with the creative director.

'Good morning, Mr Fothergill,' he said loudly.

Gordon mumbled a few words at last.

'Oh Christ. You sound terrible,' said Toby. 'Have you got a cold?'

'Yes. A very bad one.'

Later, Gordon perked up and by the middle of the afternoon the two men were flicking paper darts at each other. Toby's missiles were particularly well made, and there were volleys of laughter when one of them hit his colleague on the cheek.

'What an unpleasant man you are,' Gordon exclaimed and then pointed humorously towards an adjoining building and added, 'The chairman looking out of his window, smiling indulgently.'

The game over, true hostilities were quickly resumed when Gordon found a shabby green file of Toby's on his desk. 'What's this? Is this yours?' he asked.

Sue watched these antics and listened to these conversations from her corner. When she felt uncomfortable she began to brush real or imaginary dust off her clothes – and in extreme circumstances she actually attacked her garments with company Sellotape, sticking and unsticking it all over herself in order to rid herself of fluff.

She did not want to be a spoilsport and sometimes tried to show her good intentions by telling a sexy story. Unfortunately she only irritated Toby more by referring to love-making as 'having it off'.

My own attempts to break through Sue's reserve had failed to bear fruit. 'Are you religious, Sue?' had been met with a tart 'None of your business, William,' and I knew little of her life on any level, other than that she was, in her own words, 'middle class'.

Her telephone conversations revealed little. In fact she used the instrument most often to find out the time, in spite of the fact that there was a perfectly reliable church clock on view from the window. Gradually, however, it became apparent that there was also one particular person to whom she spoke several times a day.

'Oh, hi,' she said in a slightly strangled voice when this special friend telephoned her.

One morning in April, Sue called in from outside to say that she was ill and was taking the day off. The following day, she arrived looking solemn and announced that she was engaged to be married. The wedding itself would not take place till the end of the year when she and her fiancé had been able to save some money.

'Bob's mad keen to get a new car this year,' she explained.

Somehow or other, the work was fitted in. Sometimes Gordon was at his desk when I arrived, comfortably settled, filing his well-manicured nails or flicking through a file of letters from job applicants which would cause him to emit an occasional gasp of 'Aaagh!' as if he were in the dentist's chair. Sometimes he might be interrupted by Toby's telephone ringing and would pick it up and say, 'Not in yet. Judging by the non-presence of his coat.'

It was at such times that Gordon might chat with me. He would hold forth on contemporary musicians – 'Ringo's trying to be cool' – or enrich my knowledge of the ageing process – 'White hair goes yellow.' Sometimes he would ask me a question or two – 'How's your metabolism, William?' – and I might even try to start a dialogue on my own. 'Do you like steamed puddings?' I asked my boss one morning. 'Not much. Do you?' came the reply.

When Toby arrived – always a little late and often asking, 'Has coffee been round yet?' – there would be more general gossip, which Gordon might suddenly cut short by saying, 'Could I have a word with you, Toby?'

Sometimes, Gordon seemed in a temper, snapping at me, 'Just finish the copy quickly. Kind of very presto indeed. Admittedly, it's a lousy product,' or berating Toby about some missing documents: 'I put them on your desk.' 'You what?'

Toby got down to work slowly, sometimes reading a paperback and eating a packet of crisps. Then he would slap his thigh, chuck aside the book, face his typewriter and breathe out slowly as he contemplated some new challenge.

'I haven't woken up yet,' he might mutter and still staring hard at his typewriter, 'It's a bugger, this one.' But after several minutes' silence he began typing very fast indeed with an excited expression on his face. He was capable of taking his work very seriously and loved discussing advertising problems.

'What frightens me about this particular account,' he began, and then tried to rally the group to excel itself. 'We're trying to make the world realize that this product is on the map,' he said. 'Let's do something that will be remembered as a great national campaign.'

Then there was some sombre talk about 'the dispersal of the self-raising element' and 'the actual cooked product'.

Much of the work itself was done at meetings. These took place in account executives' offices on the floor below, in conference rooms, and sometimes further afield, in hotels or on the client's own territory.

Gordon was always running in and out with bundles of material under his arm, sometimes accompanied by a spruced-up Toby and often pursued by executives.

'I really think you'd better get to the next meeting,' the man with the pigskin briefcase warned Gordon one day.

'I'll be there in body but not in spirit,' said Gordon and the battle continued.

'Eight-thirty in the morning?' he exclaimed one afternoon. 'I shall be speaking to him severely, with rage.'

The following day he was still fuming. 'I've just received my ticket. Seven a.m. at St Pancras. God, how grim. Will there be breakfast on the train?'

A few days later another out-of-town meeting was arranged and Gordon announced that this time he would make his own travel arrangements.

'I'll be driving there,' he told the executive in charge. 'What about garaging?'

He spent a lot of time complaining about these meetings but seemed to enjoy the importance which these responsibilities assumed.

'I really must be over at the Hilton by two,' he said during an American client's visit. 'Anyhow, I've already got three meetings this afternoon.'

'That seems really almost too many,' said Fothergill.

Later, I was surprised to find Gordon lying flat on his desk, relaxing and chewing something at the same time.

'My three o'clock meeting never happened,' he murmured. 'Which made me extremely pleased.'

Gordon sometimes returned from these outings with specific news for one of us.

'Well done, William,' he had exclaimed soon after my arrival in the firm. 'Your Billy Dainty idea went down well with the account group and we're going to present it to the client.'

Now he spoke more slowly and solemnly. 'Mr Fothergill,' he said, and then paused, 'rather likes your headline.'

Often, he returned to our office somewhat crestfallen.

'Raikes says the client's reaction was neutral,' he announced one afternoon.

'Neutral?' Sue and Toby gasped in indignation.

Another time, the news was, 'Briefly, they've turned down everything.'

'Quite honestly, this is what I expected,' said Toby, who had more experience of failure.

On another occasion, the men returned in triumph.

'That was disposed of pretty quickly,' said Gordon, rubbing his hands together and lying down again on the top of his desk.

'It was the first time I've seen Fothergill in action,' said Toby. 'He was in great form.'

A few minutes later, the creative director himself burst into the room, exclaiming, 'We've got a show. We're in business.' Then he was off again, singing, 'All things bright and beautiful . . .' as he danced down the corridor.

Organizing or confirming these meetings was one of the duties of Fothergill's secretary, Louise. It was she who had glared at me on my first day, saying nothing. It was she I sometimes saw on the Underground, casting the same beady eye at her fellow-passengers. She was a surprisingly confident though humble figure who spent much of her time trying to decipher entries in Fothergill's diary or track him down in different parts of the building. Her voice often rang out from far away down the corridor.

'Can you tell me if Mr Fothergill is in Studio One?'

'Is that Mr Fothergill's house? When did he leave?'

'Sorry to keep you waiting,' she told a caller on another line. 'I'm afraid I've lost track of him.'

Then she had a brainwave.

'He may have gone to the little boys' room.'

Louise may have been the longest serving member of the creative team. For twenty-five years she had worked at the firm and once a month she buried herself, lips pursed, in the house magazine. She wore old-fashioned, well-polished shoes and had her own tea-making equipment beside her desk. Sometimes she tried to drag clients and colleagues down to her own level – offering Fothergill's visitors special cups of tea and ginger-nut biscuits. At other times, she tried to participate in the general mood on the floor, responding to proposals with, 'It seems feasible to me,' and remarking after a set-back of some sort, 'The client is a devil really.'

In the corridors, figures rushed past me, shouting, 'Hi, William!' Trolleys rattled by, little processions of staff scurried off to meetings and the chairman's stately secretary froze into immobility as an art director did a hunchback impression in the doorway of his office. In the lifts and lavatories, other dramas were played out.

Here I had further encounters with Fothergill and Raikes. A cigarette often glowed in Fothergill's mouth as he returned late from lunch, darted up the stairs and into a lavatory. He still did not acknowledge my existence but he chatted generally in the lift.

'A bloody bore having a commissionaire who doesn't know people's names,' he remarked one morning when he had been stopped entering the building.

Another morning, he protested that he had been 'wedged in a non-smoker from Woking to Waterloo'.

I could think of no response to these pronouncements and when I ventured a comment of my own, on the ugliness of a new clock that had been installed in the lift, my words fell on stony ground. 'Rather a handsome clock,' the creative director replied.

Meeting Gordon or Toby in the lift, Fothergill would be a good deal more effusive, remarking, 'That was a damned good lunch,' or 'Those shoes don't look very waterproof.'

Raikes was more withdrawn on such occasions, leaning back in a corner, fiddling in his pocket or tapping impatiently on the door with a pencil.

Gradually I got to know others in the firm. There was a pale-faced red-bearded man who often poked his head out of his office like a frightened animal. There was an untidy copywriter in another group who talked about 'going for a crap'. And in the artists' group across the corridor there was a smiling, capable art director called Sandy Scott. The latter relationship was short-lived – as Sandy Scott was soon to be sacked after a personality clash with the ambitious deputy creative director.

'Peculiar business,' murmured the stricken art director. 'Raikes worked under me at Newtons not so long ago.'

The sacking cast a strange shadow over the day which even affected our group.

'Funny atmosphere this afternoon,' remarked Toby.

'There always is when people are leaving,' said Sue.

A few days later, a secretary entered our office and said she was collecting money for a leaving present for the unfortunate art director.

'Do you know Sandy Scott?' she asked Toby.

'I do,' said Toby. 'But I don't know if I've got any change to delve into.'

These bouts of work and play were briefly interrupted by lunch hours.

At lunch-time the building was quiet for a while. Then far away in the street below you would hear cries of 'News' and 'Standard' as the early editions of the evening papers came on sale.

Much longer breaks came at weekends. On Friday mornings, several members of the staff came in with suitcases or makeshift overnight bags. Sometimes even Raikes had a hold-all with him and once I saw the word 'Eccles' scribbled on the pad under his arm.

One Friday morning, Toby arrived with a black briefcase, a paper carrier bag containing a towel, a squash racket and a cheap, old suitcase held together with string.

In spite of his commitments elsewhere and unfavourable underlying feelings, he jokingly invited Sue to come away with him to Brighton. Later, when she was out of the office, he laid into her as usual.

'Look at her today. She's frustrated at the prospect of another deadly weekend with her fiancé. That's why I suggested the dirty weekend in Brighton. Why can't she let her hair down?'

Fothergill's secretary Louise was completely unashamed of the dullness of her social life. One lunch-time she remarked, 'I always make a point of going out at lunchtime unless it's pouring with rain.' One Friday afternoon, I found her sipping a cup of tea and remarking, 'My last cup of tea until— I shall get into Wolverhampton at half-past nine tonight.'

Others were more dynamic about their plans. Toby talked about 'beetling off for the weekend' and one of the executives insisted, 'I want to get out on to the A40 before the madness.'

A great many civilities were exchanged on Friday nights.

My own husky farewells were drowned by cries of 'Cheers' and 'Have a nice weekend', sentiments which were echoed two days later with cries of 'Nice weekend?' to which the replies were equally flat. 'Not bad. Not bad at all' and 'You?'

The absence of one of the typists on a Monday morning was the subject of a wisecrack by Gordon. 'Her usual Monday morning sickness,' he laughed. 'She must have wild weekends.'

Toby's weekends were as dramatic as his weekly life.

One Monday he arrived declaring, 'I've had the most hectic weekend imaginable,' and later in the day was still out of sorts. 'I'm a bit muddled after a muddling weekend,' he said apologetically to a visiting executive.

One day in the early summer, when I had been in the firm about five months, Gordon told me one morning, 'Unless anything happens either way, you'll be on the training scheme until September.'

'Is this the normal thing?' I asked.

'Oh yes, this is the normal thing. I was on it. Only I was taken off it after two months – you see I was twenty-six, which is five years older than you.'

Meanwhile Toby was also considering his position and regularly scanning the trade magazines for news of a better job. At about this time, his eye was caught by an advertisement for a senior post in Brussels and he quickly despatched a telegram saying, 'Creative Directorship. Hold everything until you get my letter.'

The ploy worked and he was summoned for an interview at the London headquarters of the company concerned. A few days later, he telephoned a senior secretary there to enquire about his prospects.

'Do you think that's a good or bad sign? Ah, good, yes. What would be the next step? Ah, I see. That's encouraging anyhow. Thanks, Anne.'

He was already on first-name terms with this secretary and a second interview with the company was followed by another phone call to his informant.

'Could I speak to – Christ, I've forgotten her name. Clark. Mrs Anne Clark. Is that Anne Clark? It's Toby.

Hello. Any news one way or the other? Yes? It's good? Tremendous, Anne, that's very sweet of you.'

A tense period followed — 'Something's obviously wrong,' commented Sue — and further calls were made to Mrs Anne Clark. After one of these, he put the receiver down slowly and said quietly, 'This is bad,' and then snapped, 'Put that down, lad,' when I picked up the paperback he had been reading.

Eventually, he lost his patience and telephoned the office in Brussels. He said 'Splendid' and 'Pardon?' several times and seemed to be negotiating the possible size of his salary.

A few seconds later, his telephone rang and Toby explained to the firm's own international operator, 'I had an urgent call to make. I see. Yes.'

In spite of these anxieties and excitements, Toby continued to take his copywriting job seriously, fulfilling his duties and obliging Gordon, as well as launching fresh arguments about the fundamental principles of advertising, dropping out of the conversation for a while and then bouncing back into it, cigarette puffing, eyebrows arched, feet shifting in emphasis. 'The trouble with this place is there are so many dull men here,' he would say, or 'Hey, wait a moment, perhaps that idea of Fothergill's isn't too bad.'

The creative director's working methods remained a matter of enduring interest and many of our visitors had their own angle on him. 'Fothergill never wastes a moment,' said one of the executives. 'I used to come up on the same train as him from Woking — he was always First Class of course — and he was always working. He used to work very little here, dictated a few letters, went off to his club, came back later and took an early train home.'

Sometimes our conversations took a more personal turn – 'Where are you residing now, Toby?' 'I'm one of the Angels of Islington' – was quickly followed by, 'I know someone who lives near you. Sue Hamble.'

A few of these people had known Toby from his university days and he remained something of a character in their eyes.

'We had a nice evening,' said a puffy-faced man one summer morning. 'Twenty overs each. A pretty light-hearted affair. Had a couple of drinks afterwards and they were all waxing nostalgic about an innings you'd had. Ninety runs in half an hour!'

Toby took such compliments in his stride and instead asked his friend, 'Did you make any runs?'

'Didn't bat.'

Sometimes these reminiscences were at cross-purposes.

'Toby, I ran into Nick Smith the other night . . .' began the puffy-faced executive.

'Nick Smith,' Toby repeated the name thoughtfully. 'I seem to remember a silly little sports car and a hat. Terribly pleased with himself for no reason.'

While Toby waited to hear about his new job, we were told that a new lady writer called Amy would be joining our group. Toby immediately remembered that he had worked with her in another firm several years earlier.

'She's terrific,' he said. 'She's like Marlon Brando.'

When the new writer arrived at our office, she hovered outside the door for a moment before entering. From his desk, Toby shouted 'Amy!' but I could not see her. Neither could Sue, who looked grimly attentive, twiddling her ball-point pen as usual.

Presently a small, smart, stout woman slowly entered the room. Gordon made the necessary introductions and Toby went off to get coffee.

'This place works on coffee like cars work on petrol,' he said on his return.

In a lazy voice, Amy told him he was looking well.

'Do you think so? You are nice,' he said and then asked his old friend out to lunch.

She accepted his invitation and said, 'I'm starving already.'

They returned at half-past three, Toby laughing, Amy tiptoeing into the room pretending to be silent.

The following morning, Toby began to talk about a man he'd met at a party the previous weekend. 'He was twenty-four, but he looks a good thirty-four – and a raddled thirty-four. He said, "Now I'll read your future." A lot of it was surprisingly shrewd. He was on black bombers, apparently. He had no saliva in his mouth . . .'

Amy was bored by this story and said languidly, 'I just think people like that . . . you know . . . Oh, Toby, you make my blood run cold.'

Within a few hours, the new writer was yawning heavily and saying, 'If only you knew how bored I am.'

When Gordon described an advertisement she had written as 'nice' she responded ungraciously. 'They say "nice" is the most damning possible verdict.'

Gordon did not reply. A visiting executive was treated

with equal disdain. 'Yeh, well,' she drawled. 'I understand what you mean. Pardon?'

Soon she was muttering, 'I'm not trying to run this bloody account,' grumbling about Fothergill – 'He does crud on' – and hurling below-the-belt insults at Gordon. 'You go to Carnaby Street,' she said during one dispute, 'and buy your bloody clothes there.'

Toby presently changed his tune about his old colleague. 'She's an intelligent, bored woman,' he admitted.

Between Amy and Sue, a flimsy rapport was established. When Sue said something about dancing, Amy tiptoed over to her desk and whispered, 'Where do you dance?'

After some embarrassed foot-shuffling, Sue replied, 'Private dances.'

One day the two women went out to lunch together. Sue reported afterwards, 'I've never known anyone walk slower. She is an extraordinary woman.'

A few days later, someone telephoned to say that Amy was ill. Gordon took the call and said cheerily, 'Tell her we look forward to seeing her as soon as she's well enough.' To the rest of the group, he declared, 'Quite honestly, I think she's in no fit state to work at all.'

Meanwhile, Toby had been summoned to Brussels for a final interview. He left the office saying he was 'feeling lousy generally' and returned three days later telling Gordon that he had been in bed with 'a fluey cold' .

'Looks as though we both had the same thing,' said Amy, back at her desk and typing a letter to a friend.

'I've been coughing my heart out,' said Toby, whose

appearance did not bear this out. He was unusually radiant. Soon he whispered that he had more or less got the job.

'I'm absoloootly delighted,' murmured Amy. 'Sounds a really cool scene.'

Toby was triumphant. His new boss, he said, was 'a terribly pleasant man' and the working conditions were 'quite fabulous'.

He made a number of absurd, happy sounds. He banged triumphantly on the line-changer of his typewriter, and when he left the room to scrounge more coffee, he was whistling jauntily.

The job was officially confirmed in writing four days later. 'So you see,' said Toby. 'We're back in business.'

'You can do the scene today,' said Amy. 'We'll have a really nice scene. Go to Leoni's and start boozing.'

Toby broke the news to Gordon, who said, 'Congratulations. Well deserved if I may say so,' and then typed out a formal letter of resignation to Fothergill.

'This is a tremendous coup,' he said. 'One's suddenly back at the top again with a lot of money.'

Sue took this turn of events in her stride. She said merely, 'Toby didn't look permanent when he came here in November.'

Gradually the news spread. 'By the way, congratulations,' said visitors to our office, but Toby brushed aside these compliments and began to talk about the appointment rather casually, as if it was a big nuisance.

'I'm just dashing off to Brussels, that's all,' he explained. 'They want a bit of copy expertise over there.'

'Can you speak the lingo?'

'A little.'

'Don't worry. I can quite see you in a couple of months. You'll be gesticulating wildly.'

Gradually his effervescence subsided. He had several weeks left to serve in the firm – and all his old problems still confronted him.

It was to deal with these that he had begun to come in much earlier in the mornings. Most days he was now settled in by nine-thirty with coffee, cigarettes and smouldering ashtray among the litter on his desk. One day I found him sifting through a pile of used cheques while he talked to his solicitor on the telephone. 'I think I ought to speak to Wigglesworth again. I thought all the creditors had been written to.'

After a while, I realized that he had only come in to use the telephone. He made no secret of the fact that the one at his Islington flat had been cut off. It was also widely known that he was desperate for his last salary cheque.

He soon began to look scruffy again, arriving one morning in stained trousers, coarse blue sweater and tight little suede shoes, none of which, he boasted, belonged to him. He waddled around his desk, making ungainly movements. Suddenly he lurched at Amy's desk.

'Could I be frightfully rude and take a cigarette? I'm absolutely dying.'

Amy was becoming equally 'flaked out' – to use one of her own expressions – doing her nails in the office with exaggerated care and more than once leaving on her desk a tissue-wrapped matchstick which she had used for cleaning inside her ears.

No one was very surprised when Amy announced that she

was leaving – but there was general astonishment when she revealed that she had got a new job as a script editor at the BBC.

'The BBC. That's the place to work,' said a lady copywriter from next door. 'I worked for CBS. I loved it.'

There was further consternation when it was rumoured that she would be working at a vastly increased salary.

'It's only a load of old crunge,' said Amy, showing us the letter of appointment in which the financial details had been struck out. 'I'm getting three thou',' she whispered to those present.

Amy's final words to me were, 'Be confident, man. Be big.'

Toby's final words on his old friend were, 'She's too adult, and she'll have to pay for it.'

Gordon was meanwhile on the crest of a new wave. He was about to leave on a business trip to New York. His companion on this jaunt would be the executive with the pigskin briefcase. Neither of them had been to America before and they now met frequently at our office to discuss their arrangements.

'Actually, I'd like to go down to Washington,' said Gordon.
'I'm told it's exceptionally pleasant at this time of year.'

'We could hire a car.'

'Sure. Why not? Yes, that would be nice. Splendid. Okay, why not?'

'Do you know any birds in New York?'

'I could rustle up a few contacts.'

As the date of his departure grew closer, Gordon

became more and more restless, sliding through doors, biting his nails and sitting at his desk only to use the telephone.

One call was to one of his Five Friends. After mentioning the latest record by the Rolling Stones and advising his friend to 'give it a listen', he said, 'While I'm on, can I have Darlene and Denise's address in the States? Any phone numbers? No, quite.'

Another call was to his garage. 'The only thing is,' he said, 'I'm off to the States for a couple of weeks. I thought I'd leave the car with you, Mr Gummer, so you could do some more trimming on it. You know, the draught-excluders and foot-wells. I'll call you when I get back and pick up the car the following day. Thanks a lot.'

On his last day in the office, Gordon gave Sue various instructions and finally advised her, 'Tickle the clients under the chin if they get obstreperous.'

Then he turned to Toby. Toby would have left the firm by the time of Gordon's return, so the two writers would have to say goodbye now. It was an awkward moment. Toby dug one hand into the side of his head, shook hands with the other, while pivoting his body away as if to avoid too much intimacy. Gordon said in an artificial voice, 'It's been nice working with you.'

Toby's last few days at the firm were marked by a further drama.

The morning after Gordon had left, the puffy-faced executive entered the office at an early hour and asked if Toby was in.

'Not as far as I know,' said Sue.

'Well, actually, I don't think he'll be coming in,' said the man. 'He's been in a car smash.'

'Serious?' asked Sue.

'I don't know. Toby hasn't paid his phone bill. Nobody can get through to him.'

'Oh, Christ,' said Sue.

'Toby dined with us last night,' the visitor continued. 'He drove off with his girlfriend and crashed straight into a stationary lorry. They were both dragged off to hospital. All a bit nasty . . .'

For a short while, a rumour swept round the firm that one of its senior copywriters had been 'carved up in a road accident'. Then came the news that it had not been a very serious collision, and for the next day or two it was left to Sue and me to play down the incident.

'He's been in a minor car crash.'

'Not a bad one, no.'

Three days later, Toby staggered into the room supporting himself with a pair of flimsy blue hospital crutches. Leaning these against the wall, he fell into his chair.

'Is it painful?' asked Sue.

'To start with, it was absolutely excruciating. The whole front of the Triumph Herald crushed up.'

Toby soon began to make light of the affair and, indeed, compared the event quite favourably with a similar incident in France the previous year. 'What happened to me in Lille was very unfortunate. The insurance company wouldn't pay a halfpenny.'

In spite of his injuries, he was in fighting spirit. And

it was soon apparent that, even now, he had come in mainly to use the telephone.

Soon he was talking once more to the senior secretary at his new employers' London office.

'If there are any international marketing men I'd like to meet them. Great, Anne.'

Anxious enquiries about the incident were soon shrugged off.

'How's the girlfriend?' asked Fothergill. 'Up and about and hiding behind dark glasses, I suppose?'

'No, everything's been patched up and all is well,' he said. 'Oh yes, she's got two lovely black eyes and a bruise on her forehead. Pardon? Yes, it was a bit of a shock.'

His remaining few days were spent mainly on the telephone arranging his departure, booking double First Class couchettes to Brussels and arranging the transportation of 'about five hundred books and a few personal effects'.

In a stream of other calls he pleaded with his many friends to keep in touch.

'I'm going on Saturday. This next Saturday. For goodness sake keep in touch, Shirley ... Come over to Brussels for Christ's sake ... Why don't you come and have a cup of tea at my club? Why don't you jump into a taxi and come over here now? ... Actually, John, I was hoping to tempt you to dinner before I left ... I'd quite like to see Sarah again in a funny sort of way ... Did she ever get her novel published? Oh, what a shame! ... One wonders how long Hong Kong's going to be with us, that's all.'

One afternoon, the puffy-faced man with whom Toby had dined on the night of the accident called in again.

'I was going to ring up and say thanks for a marvellous meal,' said Toby gallantly.

'Can I give you a hand?' asked the visitor as Toby struggled to his feet.

Money matters continued to preoccupy him and were occasionally mentioned in his telephone conversations. 'I bank at Barclays in the – Christ, where is it? What I'll do, Jimmy, is when I get to Brussels, I'll shoot some money over to you.'

There was a final set-back on his last day in the office when he received his pay-slip. Largely due to various prolonged international calls earlier in the month, in addition to certain advance loans he had been given, his pay had been docked by nearly half. On receiving this news he began breathing deeply and then humming.

'How's Billy Dainty?' he asked suddenly.

Soon he was summoned down the corridor to Fothergill's office, from which he was to emerge in high spirits.

'A charming man,' he said. 'I'd forgotten how charming he is. He's given me some introductions in Brussels.'

When that evening he finally quit the office, he had dispensed with his crutches but was heavily laden with files, papers, a red-lined mackintosh, the reefer jacket, a hospital blanket and other possessions. After offering me a hearty farewell, he hitched up his trousers.

'You couldn't open the door for me, could you?'

A moment later, Sue and I faced each other across the empty office. I soon began to miss Toby, but Sue wasted no time in expressing her contempt for him.

'He had no impact,' she said as if describing an advertisement. 'He was a waster. I have no wish to see him again.'

Sue and I now briefly enjoyed the office to ourselves.

'Begin again. Slowly,' she said, when I began grumbling about the task in hand.

'I can't do it,' I said eventually.

'Well, then, give it back to me and I'll give you something else.'

Later, I asked her about her mother and father and endeavoured to interest her in my own family background, furnishing her with details such as the names of our family dogs.

'The youngest one is called Candy,' I said brightly.

'That's very interesting,' she replied.

A few minutes later, she had had quite enough of this repartee and snapped, 'Let me work, William.'

It was not long before Gordon was back from America, bounding into the room wearing a new pair of dark glasses.

'Christ, you're back,' said a visiting executive. 'Was it all very high-powered?'

'Fantastic,' said Gordon several times.

'Did you and Denis go round together?'

'Not all the time.'

'What super glasses,' said Sue.

'They are rather, aren't they?'

Gordon then bounded off for a meeting with Raikes. He returned clapping his hands and announcing that he had found an ideal replacement for Toby – 'a nervous but brilliant Australian' who had worked for the Seltzer Agency in Chicago and had just arrived in England from Italy.

This new senior writer appeared in our office a few days later. His name was Peter, he was about thirty years old and had spent most of his adult life in America. Pale and hungry-looking, he had white eyelashes and short cropped ginger hair. His thin American suit was tightly buttoned around him. Gordon shouted the introductions as if compering a variety show.

'And this is William!' he said finally.

When later that morning Fothergill was in the office 'nattering' – one of his own expressions – Gordon suddenly pounded forward and introduced him to Peter. Fothergill's face split into a smile and he showed his strong white teeth as he quickly shook hands.

It was soon obvious that the newcomer was broke. He made no secret of the fact that he needed an immediate advance. Gordon assured him that this was easily organized and told him to contact Mr Potter, the personnel manager.

Peter then began typing a five-paragraph letter explaining his plight. Mr Potter replied to this within minutes, not only arranging the requested advance but also offering him a private loan. 'If you are in a spot, I can let you have some cash.'

'Potter's so nice,' said Gordon. 'Always doing that sort of thing.'

Peter's next stammered question concerned accommodation. 'Do you know any flat or room-letting agencies?'

'How expensive?' asked Sue.

'No, not too expensive. I'll get it from an agency. I hate walking around. Are they state-run?'

He began telephoning and muttering, 'I really want to get fixed up tonight. Single room with kitchen.'

He soon discovered a place in Pimlico and made a phone call to the landlord.

'What if my girlfriend wants to stay overnight?' he asked in a trembling voice.

By the end of the first day, Peter had begun rebuilding his life. He had placed a number of businesslike calls to company officials – 'I am at present on an emergency tax code' – and had also sampled the firm's beverages. 'I don't know what's worse here, the tea or the coffee.'

The next day, Peter appeared in the same thin suit and immediately telephoned someone.

'I just get out of the subway, stagger a hundred yards and I'm here. Yeh, I'll be able to lie in longer in the mornings now.'

Then he swivelled round and began typing very fast, his body locked into the desk. After a while, he paused and, with eyes narrowing, read over what he had typed, scribbling alterations as he went along. When he dropped his pencil and bent double to pick it up, the manoeuvre emphasized the thinness of his pelvis.

A meeting took place later in our office. While Gordon and an executive argued, Peter hung his head, twiddled his fingers and gazed forward at a page of doodles.

In spite of this jellified non-participation, Peter was quickly incorporated into the system and accepted as a nice,

ordinary guy. When he left at night, there were cries of
'Okay, cheers, Pete. See you,' but his face was scowling as
he left the building, and his collar turned up.

Peter understood office routine, turned out advertising
slogans rapidly, had considerable typewriter know-how,
could blow perfect smoke rings and was fussed over by
women.

'Your nose wrinkles when you laugh,' remarked a
typist.

'Cute or not?' he replied.

One afternoon I picked up his telephone and a soft
foreign voice said, 'Peter?'

Peter's first few days in the firm were spent slinking in and
out of the office, sheepish and shorn. 'I'm just going to the
men's room,' he would explain, or 'I'm just going to buy
an umbrella.'

When asked his name, he gave it in an apologetic,
doubtful tone.

'He really is a terribly introverted boy,' commented
Sue.

The complexities of Peter's life were soon underlined
by a number of disturbing telephone calls from Italy, where
his wife still remained.

'Jesus! Baby! Can you hear now? Baby, look. Do you
want to come here in two weeks? I can send you the fare.
Ah, please don't get upset. It's terrible.'

He thumbed through the contents of his wallet while
he spoke.

A less frantic call followed to a London publisher's
office.

'I'm calling about a novel I sent to your company two months ago. Yes. It's been quite a long time . . . Thank you. Ah, Mr Woolf, I was wondering if you located that typescript . . .' he began in a trembling voice.

Turning to me, he then said, 'Pathetic sight?'

Within a day or two, tiny intangible bonds had been established between Peter and me. The newcomer's staccato movements, deftness, various demands and commands – 'Show me,' he said spotting a book on my desk – were combined with references to my 'scarecrow form' and 'parchment skin', which for some reason I took as complimentary.

'You are the only person I can speak to here,' he told me and he would often cross the room, dig me in the ribs with his index finger and hand me a slip of paper on which he had written, 'Hell is other people,' 'Imagination is the highest form of intelligence,' or some other intimacy.

He soon revealed that all his property was in a 'House of Credit' in Italy and he was already seeking an evening job to make ends meet. 'I'll get a job as a cleaner,' he said. 'I hate dealing with people.'

It was not long before more bitter confidences were passing across the floor of the office. Peter then spoke of his failure as a writer – 'I am the greatest novelist in England at the moment, completely unknown, unsuspected and laughed at' – and as a husband. His girlfriend, whose existence was unknown to his wife, had now left London for Paris. He had nearly collapsed on Victoria Station after seeing her off and then gone back to his bed-sitting-room and cooked spaghetti in a kettle.

'I almost threw myself out of the window. I went to bed the most depressed man in London.'

As far as the firm was concerned, he disliked almost everybody.

'That guy gives me the shits,' he remarked after a meeting with Raikes and he was equally dismissive of the creative director. 'He's garrulous, loquacious,' he said after Fothergill had held court in our office, enthusing about 'Antibes, years and years ago . . .' and, God, what fun he'd had in Scotland as a boy. Gordon's fashionable clothes were, he said, 'complete conformity'. One weekend he had seen our boss in a Chelsea supermarket – 'wearing a phoney leather jacket with a high-powered camera strapped round his neck'. Sue, he described as, 'the most screwed-up woman he'd ever met'. One of the executives who visited us he branded 'a fruit'.

'If only I could get a job where I could work at home and not go to bloody meetings,' he moaned, but there was no evidence that his time outside the office was any happier than his working hours. One morning, he revealed that he had spent the previous evening wandering around World's End looking at the generators for the Underground. Another morning, he complained that all the pictures he had stuck on the wall of his bed-sittingroom had been taken down by the landlord.

In the office he would occasionally brighten up and might even feel inspired to crack a simple joke. Gordon would chuckle loudly, then softly. Sue would murmur, 'I like that,' and go back to her work. In return, Peter would snort or croak at any witticisms that Gordon or Sue had to share. My own attempts at humour were less politely received. 'Oh, Jesus,' he said of one offering, 'that isn't funny at all.'

Such moments of hostility were followed by warm exchanges, flattery was followed by mockery and my own overtures were sometimes met by coolness, primness or weird smiles.

'You really ought to see a psychiatrist about your inferiority complex,' Peter muttered one afternoon, and when I asked if I could see what he was writing, he replied, 'Naah, it's a personal letter.'

He then added more brutally, 'I didn't ask you to latch on to me like this.'

In spite of these ups and downs, I remained impressed by Peter's experience of the world and delighted by his literary aspirations – I, too, had ideas of being a writer – and when one lunch-time I spotted my new colleague's closely cropped head and padded white mackintosh moving through the crowds in Leicester Square, I quickly caught up with him and we walked back to the office together.

One day, a large parcel arrived from Italy and was placed on Peter's desk. He opened it in the office and spread out some of the garments it contained without embarrassment. They were variously marked 'Made in the USA', 'Science in Fashion', 'Wash Wear Dacron Cloth' and 'Fashions from the Ends of the Earth'.

'Got a clothes parcel,' he remarked.

'You did? Great!' Gordon replied and then added the word, 'Relief!'

A few days later, a letter from France was also placed

on his desk, which Peter read with a rapidly darkening expression on his face.

That afternoon, he revealed to me that his girlfriend in Paris was pregnant.

'I'm unlucky,' he fumed. 'That's all it is. When this happened in Chicago I knew the city, I had a car. She doesn't even know a doctor . . . I've never had a scrap of fucking luck at any time in my life, except getting a job in advertising.'

While he was talking, Fothergill's secretary Louise trotted into the room and came up to him.

'Do you want the stamp on that letter I put on your desk this morning?'

Peter also discussed the crisis with one of the art directors, with whom he had established a certain rapport.

'Send her some money, Pete, and don't give it another thought,' was the offered advice and in due course I saw my colleague in the queue at the local Post Office, with a small registered package in his hand. He looked like a spoilt child.

A few days later, Peter's problems took on an extra dimension, when his wife arrived from Italy and moved into his bed-sitter. On her first morning she rang him at the office.

'Tea and toast eleven shillings?' he cried. 'Where was this? Look, don't go out again till I teach you the money. A steak costs ten shillings. Tea costs about one shilling.'

During the next few weeks I took several anxious messages from Peter's wife – 'Will you have him call me?' – and her presence in London became known to visitors to our office.

'How does she like it over here, Pete?'

'She's not looking forward to the winter.'

'There's not much you can do about that.'

Peter and I occasionally had lunch together. My friend had quickly tired of a café I knew well up the road – 'I don't want to go to that coffee lounge ever again' – and steered me instead to a pub he had discovered – 'You get a beautiful steak for seventeen-and-six and the most beautifully cooked French fries.' Here, the elasticity of my bread roll spun some butter across the room and Peter talked excitedly about life's possibilities.

'We could be flying off to Nice at three o'clock this afternoon,' he said, slamming his hand down on the table.

Then our conversation turned to his marriage. 'I was really screwed up before I met Lottie,' he told me – and, 'Lottie's a much nicer person than I am. No, really, not kidding.'

Another lunch-time, he said, 'Lottie's saving up money to leave me – to go back to America. She'll be happy as soon as we're separated again.' He then disclosed that he had formed a new interest in a girl who worked in a bank near the office.

'It's ridiculous,' he said, explaining that he had so far resisted her advances. 'She's absolutely dying, dying . . .'

Meanwhile, news of my former colleague had reached the firm. According to an executive who had been in Brussels on business, Toby was not at all happy there.

'It's far more expensive than he expected. He's living

in a very small apartment and he's not exactly painting the town red.'

This revelation coincided with an enquiry from the office manager, Mr Potter, about Toby's present whereabouts.

'It's about a private phone call he made on his last morning. We've sent him three reminders but he hasn't paid yet.'

In October, another alien figure joined our group, also Australian.

'Who's that?' asked Gordon entering the office. 'I'm sorry, what is your name? Sorry? Oh, super!'

The newcomer's name was Flynn. He was twenty-two years old and a tough little nut of a man. His hair was short and grizzly and he had a gnome's smile. All his clothes were Australian – he had only left his homeland a few weeks earlier – and these garments contrasted sharply with Peter's natty formal American attire. He wore ill-fitting green trousers, hoiked up by braces, leather cowboy boots and a tan cardigan.

He spoke extremely softly and typed very fast with a superbly light touch, often with a cigarette hanging out of his mouth in the cowboy style.

Sue appeared to have taken an instant dislike to him. 'How I hate men who wear cardigans,' she murmured.

Peter was marginally more tolerant. 'They're all like that just after they've left. Very provincial. I haven't been there for ten years.'

There was a certain exuberance to Flynn, however, which Peter lacked. His regrets about leaving Australia –

'I'm sad about not seeing my nephew grow up' – were outweighed by his delight with England and everything it offered. His favourite author, he said, was Len Deighton – 'bloody clever' – and even the English weather – 'I've had to wear a jumper every day' – did not upset him. He got up each day in a bouncy form – 'My breakfast takes two minutes flat' – and had already been 'horse-riding' in Richmond Park: as it happened, he had fallen off – the muscular legs which protruded from the leather boots were covered in bruises – but he was thrilled by the experience.

He and Peter soon exhausted their mutual Australian interests but established a healthy give and take. One Friday afternoon, Flynn asked his fellow-countryman, 'Got a big weekend lined up?' Peter replied, 'No, very small.' When Peter left the office forty minutes early, Flynn hissed at him.

My own dealings with Flynn were slightly combative – 'I've scored a bull's eye!' 'No you haven't. You said nothing' – but between Flynn and Gordon an unexpected friendliness had sprung up. I soon became aware of funny, clenched communicating smiles and grunts being exchanged between the two men.

'Flynn brings out the worst in Gordon,' Peter muttered.

One of the newcomer's charms for Gordon was that he was able to make a wide variety of highly realistic bird noises.

Within a few weeks the intimacy between the two was such that Flynn had started putting his feet up on Gordon's desk while Gordon was actually writing at it. Far from discouraging this effrontery, Gordon seemed to welcome it and wanted to see more of Flynn outside the office. Soon he was fixing an actual date.

'Bring a bird. I'll bring Jill and we'll have a meal at the Terrazza.'

The friendship was to reach a high point a few days later.

One morning Flynn suddenly made an oblique announcement.

'Tomorrow is air pistol day. Friday is slaughter day.'

'What do you mean?' I asked.

'This bloody pigeon who arrives outside my window at five-thirty every morning.'

'Are you going to kill it?'

'I'm not going to kill it, but I'm going to scare the shit out of it. If every time he lands on the window-sill he gets a pellet up the arse, sooner or later he'll learn not to do it. It's called condition reflex . . .'

The following day, Flynn telephoned to establish that he had enough money in his bank and then went out and bought an air pistol.

Sue winced in her corner as he unwrapped the brown paper parcel and began to assemble his purchase, oiling and handling it, and peering through its sights.

Sucking on a cigar-style cigarette, which he held as if it really was a cigar, he then took imaginary aim round the office. Suddenly Gordon bounced in.

'How about that?' said Flynn showing off the gun and giving it a final affectionate wipe at the same time.

At first Gordon merely smiled politely but soon he began to show unbridled interest in the new toy.

The gun fired both pellets and tiny feathered darts – the latter were soon being shot across the office in all directions, hitting the holiday postcards on the noticeboard with a smack. Sue soon chose to leave the room but Peter, after mumbling something about 'total antipathy', suddenly forgot his problems and joined in the fun.

'Keep still, William,' the marksmen shouted as they began to pepper a poster a few inches above my head. Gordon was now the ringleader, waddling to and fro, swivelling his tightly tailored torso in all directions, holding the gun with two hands, lowering it slowly from the ceiling before firing and then rushing forward to remove the darts from the target.

The gun also interested several of the visitors to our office.

'We'll have to go blasting one night,' an executive told Flynn. 'At the Kensington Rifle and Pistol Club.'

Without warning, the firm now underwent a violent convulsion. To cries of 'Shit!', 'Christ!' and 'Well, well, well!' a vigorous re-shuffling took place. 'Any questions?' asked the chairman at a big meeting. 'Nobody want to know anything?' Gordon was promoted and his group disbanded, the tea ladies were replaced with vending machines and, at long last, Fothergill was sacked – or retired to grow rhododendrons. Raikes grabbed his job – and a tall, elegant, floppy figure called Mr Meek took over as administrator of our floor.

'Good morning, good morning,' said this weird intruder, welcoming us back to our reorganized offices like a head waiter and then turning to his secretary, saying,

'Thank you, m'dear,' and beginning to concentrate on the furnishings of his own little den, already adorned with plants, watering can, silk cushions and a small tree. 'I told Potter I must have a carpet in here and he said "Fine".'

At lunch-time that day, as more and more protests about the new arrangements flowed in, Mr Meek remarked, 'I must get me a bullet-proof jacket.'

During the days that followed, I had one final silent encounter with Fothergill in the lift. He wore a short army coat and carried a battered crocodile-skin briefcase. His lips were firmly set but he looked rattled and angry at last.

He got out at the ground floor and dashed across the reception area and out into the street. In an unnecessarily loud voice, he yelled for a taxi and stopped one immediately. Some workmen on a neighbouring building site were bemused by his urgency and one of them shouted 'Wheeee!' as the vehicle sped off with its impatient passenger on board.

I eventually learned that I was to be moved to a dingy room at the back of the building. After enjoying for many months the prestige of working mainly on ideas for television commercials, I had been demoted to write pack copy, shelf strips and point-of-sale material. My new supervisor was the red-bearded man whose wrinkled timid face I had occasionally seen in the corridor. His name was Robin Peacock and he had worked in advertising for thirty years.

'Come in,' he said. 'Squat down.'

Packing cases containing files surrounded us.

'It's like Grand Central Station,' quipped Robin.

'Anybody for putting a stink-bomb in the housemaster's study?'

Then he briefed me on my first job, a trade advertisement for poultry grit.

'Feel free to do anything you damn well want,' he urged me, and then added in only half-jocular style, 'Well, don't just stand there!'

My new boss was soon on the telephone. 'Is that the switchboard? Peacock here. This is in pursuit of an earlier call . . .'

I had been given a desk near my new boss and alongside another writer – a shrimp of a girl called Lizzie, who had big heavily made-up eyes and brightly painted fingernails.

I had seen this girl trip-trip-tripping along the corridor in pink pants and wondered what her job was. Robin seemed in awe of her. He described her as 'a bit of fluff' and believed that she lent a touch of glamour to his new group.

On her first morning, Lizzie spent much of her time chattering on the telephone about her flat-sharing plans.

'Pat's beginning to feel a bit dubious. That leaves Maggie and Sal. Everything's getting a bit crowded at Claremont Drive . . . Hold on a moment while I grab a match . . . Look,' she said suddenly, 'I'd better get back as Robin was having words with me when the telephone rang.'

The red-bearded Robin had begun to look uncomfortable in his corner but was too timid to say anything other than, 'I'm not too keen on your taking personal calls here.' His lifetime in advertising had made him an authority on the subject but he was too shy to throw his weight around.

Over the years he had developed some odd little habits. He talked to himself at his desk. After gulping down a beaker of machine coffee on the first morning, he opened a drawer in his desk, took out a lump of sugar and popped it into his mouth. After lunch I found him bent over behind his desk examining his light brown trousers and Hush Puppies. 'It's all right, thanks. Just a few grease spots. I had fried chicken for lunch and splashed myself a bit.'

Others in the group had more gumption. There was a big middle-aged art director named Buckingham, who burst into the office saying, 'Heavenly morning!' stripped down to his shirt-sleeves and strode around carrying his spectacles and complaining about his workload. 'I spend half my time answering bloody invoices!'

There were also two designers, Geoff and John, who were soon plodding away at their table by the window, either sketching out advertisements, working with Cow Gum and Letraset or talking quietly on the telephone. On the first morning, I heard Geoff re-establishing contact with one of his mates. 'First things first,' he began. 'I'm on the same telephone number and extension number. Right. Now, how are things?' 'Twenty-three minutes to opening time!' his colleague shouted an hour or two later, but as the day wore on I realized that Buckingham had the team under his thumb.

'Oh, look everybody, he's been to Harry Fenton's and bought some tight-fitting trousers,' he exclaimed when John returned from lunch, and he was equally assertive when he found Lizzie lingering in the office at the end of the day.

'Aren't you going home, Lizzie?'

'I'm waiting for a phone call.'

'Aren't you on the phone at home?'

The remaining member of the group was a secretary called Nancy. 'I'm a bit dozy today, a bit dozier than usual,' she had declared on the first morning, but her skirt was tightly belted and she knew how to fight for herself. 'Chuckle, chuckle, chuckle,' she said when people made fun of her, and when I exclaimed, 'Nancy, you're not in the new phone book!' she replied, 'Cut to the quick, William, I really am.'

The next morning, when I entered the office and said, 'Hello, Nancy,' there was a brief pause followed by, 'Beg your pardon, William?'

My old colleagues, especially Toby, were already a million miles away and seemed towering figures compared to my new companions. I saw little of Gordon. My occasional encounters with him in the corridor were rather disconcerting. 'Any news of Toby?' I asked and then, 'Is it possible to get through Robin Peacock's façade?'

'Façade?' he responded to the second question primly. 'He hasn't got one. He's just a nice, ordinary bloke.'

'What's this eau-de-cologne you wear?' I enquired another time.

'It's – oh, I can't remember. It's very expensive.'

One day in the lift, Gordon was talking about his car to an executive.

'The only thing is it's tending to spit back into the carburettor when it's cold.'

'Keeping your tan well,' remarked the executive. 'Is it the good old infra-red every night?'

'No,' said Gordon. My former group head had then attended to his hair with two different combs and waltzed off looking as buoyant as ever.

Sue, now a married woman, was even more elusive. Sometimes I glimpsed her swinging down the corridor like a soldier, saw her pirouetting in the reception area, or rushing up a staircase without slowing down when she spotted me.

One afternoon, when she and I were temporarily trapped together at the coffee machine, she lashed out, 'Are you as loony as ever?'

Flynn I also saw little of. Like me, he had been allocated to a deadbeat group and when we occasionally passed each other in the corridor, he simply said, 'I'm getting out of here. Pressed for his opinion of the new regime, he simply said, 'Stinks.' Cut off from Gordon, he was completely deflated and a few weeks later I learned that he was returning to Australia.

Peter and I remained in touch, however. He had done well out of the reshuffle, had been promoted to copy chief and given a salary increase. We met momentarily in the corridor – split-second encounters – and sometimes his wiry arm grabbed me in the street outside the office.

On one such occasion he told me he had now caught a disease from the girl in the bank. 'She turned out to be a nymphomaniac,' he tut-tutted. 'I've only slept with two women this year. One got pregnant. The other gave me a dose.'

Peter would reveal a certain amount about his life and then cut out and become defensive. Some evenings he would arrange to call on me at home. Other times he would leave the building without a word and I would watch him hurry off up the pavement, cross the sunlit street and disappear into the Underground station.

'Okay? Good,' said the sleek Mr Meek emerging one afternoon from the new creative director's office. Raikes had had his hair cut much shorter. He looked thinner and scraggier, his voice had a new twang and he wore an even more monstrous pair of spectacles.

Once I passed his open door and saw him standing on one foot doing his expenses. Later, I heard him on the telephone to Moss Bros about hiring a wedding outfit. On another occasion the door was closed and I heard the sound of a heavy filing cabinet being dragged across the room. He remained an elusive and unpopular figure.

'You know what he's like,' grumbled an executive. 'As slippery as a bloody orange pip.'

'Nobody likes Raikes,' said one of the typists.

This included Louise, the secretary he had inherited from Fothergill.

'Don't walk away, Mr Raikes, while I'm talkin' to you,' I heard her protest. 'Should I write "entertain you to lunch" or "have you to lunch"?'

'Yes, sure,' was Raikes's unhelpful reply.

'You're being obtuse, Louise,' I heard him say later. 'You're being deliberately obtuse.'

Louise took the new job in her stride, however, introducing herself proudly as 'Mr Raikes's sec-et-terry', continuing to brew tea and coffee on her own equipment and to hold forth about her sister's home in Wolverhampton – 'well, just outside Wolverhampton'. She also continued to make observations on the weather. 'There's a howling gale out there,' she reported one afternoon and then reflected, 'It can rain its bloomin' head off, it doesn't affect me. Unless it's lunch-time or going-home time.'

Life in the new group offered few amusements. Robin Peacock was hardly ever absent from his desk and took only brief lunch hours. On one special occasion he took the afternoon off to give a lecture to 'a bunch of undergraduates' and another day he announced that he had to go and have a 'flu shot', but otherwise his wrinkled brow was always there behind his typewriter, at which he would begin tapping the moment he returned to the office.

Buckingham could be quite critical of other people's time-keeping – 'What a shambles! Comes breezing in at ten to ten without an apology!' – but he did not hesitate to make full use of Robin's rare absences. On the day of the undergraduates lecture, I heard the art director quickly booking 'a table for two' at Stone's Chop House and then leaving the office with a whisper that he could be back 'about a quarter past four'.

He also had more legitimate excuses for taking time off, remarking one quiet afternoon, 'Robin, I'm going home as I have a migraine,' and then telephoning his wife and saying, 'Oh, hello. I'm coming home as I have a slight migraine.' Another day, he telephoned to say, 'I want to pick up a suit for pressing, darling. I thought I'd come back at lunch-time.'

Life plodded on with few other diversions. One morning, it was announced that Robin's copy of *Early American Advertising Art* had been 'nicked overnight' from the shelf behind his desk. My colleague Lizzie continued to drift about the office, her heels hitting the floor, occasionally making an inane laugh or screeching, 'You nit! You fool!' or to me in particular, and a good deal more venomously, 'Oh, shut up, William!'

My dealings with Robin had also become frayed.

'You have theories on everything,' he said nervously and to some of my observations and queries could only reply, 'Er . . . I see.'

Finally, he said flatly, 'I think you're crackers.'

The secretary Nancy remained more amiable. Sometimes she got involved in long private telephone calls, during which she spoke very little in a very soft voice, and sometimes she moaned about her health – 'I may end up a record-holder. Longest cold ever' – but most of the time she jumped about making willing remarks. 'Just a moment, I'll get a pad' or, 'I'll fly and get some coffee.'

In the absence of tea ladies, Nancy had taken upon herself to fetch beverages for us all from the vending machines near the lift. Twice a day, she would arrive with a tray full of steaming drinks.

'Nobody has chocolate except for me?' I asked.

'No, Geoff does occasionally,' Nancy replied.

Geoff was the 'doggie' of the group, a faithful character who wore the same shoes, socks, 'Dalecraft' trousers and jacket everyday and accepted orders from Buckingham good-naturedly.

'Okay, Buck. Will do,' he said, 'I'll whip it over to the client Monday morning.'

He also found time to do freelance work on the side and drove a tough bargain in the process. Cupping both his hands to the telephone, he said in a low voice, 'He must be prepared to pay me a professional fee. Otherwise I'd just be doing him a favour.'

His less robust colleague, John, accepted orders less graciously. 'Charming!' he said on being given a difficult last-minute task, and the following morning complained that it had kept him in the office till half-past nine at night – to which Geoff responded by saying, 'Oh, crikey.'

The two designers offered each other cigarettes – Geoff sometimes hiding one he was about to light in order to accept a free one from his colleague – but there was no gossip, or small talk, or philosophizing, such as had diverted the previous group, while these cigarettes were consumed.

If there was any conversation at all, it was restricted to advertising matters. Once I heard the two men discussing the merits of a new typeface.

'The cap M is the ugly sod in the family,' said John.

Another day they deliberated over a layout that needed the client's urgent approval.

'Put it on the one-o'clock van,' said Geoff.

'Can't,' replied his colleague. 'Still got gubbins on it.'

Weekends passed almost unnoticed and without comment.

'Nice weekend, Robin?' I might enquire.

'Quite nice,' he would reply. 'Quite nice, indeed.'

Lizzie was the only person present who cared to share her life with anyone else.

'I crept back to town about ten o'clock,' she announced after a weekend in Brighton. 'Mick was sitting in the only comfy chair in the lounge.'

A few days later, Lizzie's domestic life seemed to have

become intolerable. 'At least half a bottle of whisky and gin had been syphoned off,' she told a caller. 'I cannot stay in that flat a moment longer because the atmosphere is so ghastly.'

The visitors to our office were also of a humble breed.

Surly messengers stood in our doorway, asking in a take-it-or-leave-it manner, 'Buckingham? Buckingham?'

Executives like dodgy schoolmasters shuffled into the room, found Robin on the telephone and muttered that they would come back later.

Others expressed surprise to find Robin present – 'I thought you were on holiday' 'I am really' – or acted unusually matey with us. 'Are you a married man, William?' asked a man with a wallet and pen in his back trouser pocket. 'What do you do at weekends, William?'

Occasionally, the new administrator Mr Meek sailed into the room and said, 'A few things I need to know, Robin,' but the new creative director seemed to take pains to avoid our backwater.

Later in the spring, the whole firm's attention was momentarily focused on our group. This was nothing to do with our work but was due to the sudden disappearance without trace of the typist Nancy.

'She seemed so conscientious,' said Robin, who took this unresolved mystery personally and looked even more worried than usual for several weeks.

'What's happened to our Nance?' the designers asked each other.

At Easter that year, Robin Peacock collapsed with a burst ear-drum and his group was disbanded. I was put to work alongside Peter again. In spite of his increasing grumpiness, he had been further promoted and I sometimes heard his name being summoned on the firm's new Tannoy system. He now had an office of his own, partitioned off within his new group, with its own door. Behind this door you could hear him typing or murmuring on the telephone. He dispatched his advertising work as quickly as possible – 'Okay? Solved?' – and supervised the group's work with mounting irritation.

'What do you want me to read it for?' he asked when I showed him some copy. 'Typographical errors?' Much of his time was spent working on his own private writings, which I heard him typing rapidly behind the frosted glass door.

My new colleagues included two writers called Fanny and Frank. Both drank heavily during the daytime – propping up the bar in the pub across the road for hours at a time.

Fanny was always heavily made up and seemed to be subject to various highs and lows. Sometimes she sailed serenely into the office, saying, 'Good morning, Frank. Good morning, Peter,' and then, 'Goody, goody,' as she read a message on her desk. Other days she seemed to be in a panic.

'I've no time. Friends round last night. Window-cleaner this morning,' she said as she removed her bright yellow coat and hung it up facing the wall.

'Nice weekend, Fan?' asked Frank another time.

'The dog was ill. Have you ever tried to give a dog medicine?'

One summer morning, she sailed in and declared,

'They're rioting in Paris. It's pouring in the south of France. It's all a mess,' but became more seriously downcast a few minutes later when men arrived to lay a carpet in Peter's little office.

'Fanny's so jealous she can hardly speak,' said Peter flicking biscuit crumbs off his desk.

Fanny took it out on the typist instead, screaming, 'You're here to do a job!' to which the typist simply replied, 'So?'

Stalking back to her desk after this incident, Fanny looked very sad. Frank was a much calmer individual. He had blackened teeth, dandruff and, when I first joined the group, a sty on each eye but he was an amiable man with an easygoing nature.

'I'm just going to wander across the road and have a drink with Fanny,' he would say at about noon and would then remain in the pub till closing time and beyond.

The two writers knew each other well and their desk-top exchanges, interspersed by long silences while they worked, reflected their familiarity.

'The heart is a lonely hunter,' remarked Frank.

'You can say that again,' said Fanny.

'This is the sort of morning people commit suicide,' said Frank a few minutes later.

'Well, I've already done so,' said his colleague.

These confessions were sometimes interrupted by the fast footsteps and flattering words of Mr Meek – 'Very splendid. Approve of that' – or by more sinister interventions from the new creative director. 'I must have a word with you sometime,' or 'I didn't see you yesterday. I want to see you today.'

To me, Raikes would simply declare, eyes bulging, 'We must exploit you more.'

Punctuality had become the creative director's new obsession — and perhaps with good reason.

The two writers were skilled at taking off the maximum amount of time and had endless excuses. One morning Fanny rang to say she was ill — 'an off risotto' — and Frank's excuse another morning was a 'cricked neck'. Peter was also getting more and more daring in this area. Soon he took off two whole days, claiming he had 'yellow throat' .

'He's gone to Paris to see a girl,' whispered Frank.

'I knew something was up,' said Fanny.

The following week, Peter bustled into the office and reluctantly resumed his responsibilities. 'Jesus, Jesus,' he muttered as he sifted through a stapled bunch of job applications from would-be copywriters. Then he diffidently telephoned an executive on the floor below. 'Oh, ah, could you ask him to come up before he goes? Oh, Jesus.'

With me he was more confident. 'Don't worry about that,' he said, handing me a long letter from a client. 'It's horse-shit.'

There was the usual team of designers attached to the group. These men occasionally smiled at me as if I was mad but showed a certain curiosity as well — 'Where are you living? Chelsea? How do you manage that?' In spite of their occasional coarse language they were a timid breed, far less daring about long lunch hours and invented illnesses. They arrived early in the morning, slung their wads of sandwiches into a drawer and slapped their cigarette packs down on their desk tops. They wore the usual brown-coloured clothes and gossiped among themselves while they worked.

'Lloyd George was a lecher. He had birds galore.'

'She's moaning like mad at the moment because we haven't got a car.'

'I was paper-hanging till one a.m.'

'Some friends of my mum own a pub down there.'

'Raikes is a cunt!'

Sometimes their ribaldry was aimed in my direction and remarks like 'William hasn't got a clue', 'Another gem from William' and 'Damn your guts, William' floated across the office.

They also made many telephone calls, planning their holidays well in advance and keeping in touch with old college friends.

'Then there's the baby. Do you think she'd need a berth as such?'

'Where are you? Oh, great. Sorry I haven't written, mate.'

Peter got on well with these men, occasionally told jokes for their benefit, or expressed astonishment at the long hours they worked.

'When did you finish last night?'

'Nine o'clock.'

'You're kidding.'

'I'm not kidding.'

As Peter's time-keeping became increasingly slapdash, these men faithfully fended off enquiries on his behalf. 'Hello, Pete's phone. No, he's in a meeting.'

Between Peter and the art director, a jovial fellow

named Roger, an irritating bond was established. They shared a keen interest in French films and I soon found them closeted in Peter's office.

'There's a terrific point where they do a dance in the café. Remember that?' said Peter.

'It's a great movie but you can't see it properly on the TV screen,' said Roger.

Later that day, Peter reassured me by confiding, 'The thing is, I've sat in offices like this, talking to people like this, for ten years . . .' and back among his designers, in the outer office, the art director was soon shouting, 'Cut that music out, will you?' and 'Do you want my elegantly styled boot in your groin?'

Roger remained a popular figure, laughing and chuckling, and it came as a great surprise to everyone when suddenly he was sacked.

'He was in there like cement,' muttered Peter.

Shortly after this shock, Raikes appeared in his shirt-sleeves and tried to reassure everyone by saying, 'Onwards, onwards, onwards. You're doing stout work, William.'

In spite of these reassurances, the nervousness in our corner of the firm increased. The voice of the creative director twanged through my head and his lopsided face and heavy-lidded eyes haunted me even when he was far away.

Once I heard him talking on the telephone to one of his own children – 'Is Mummy there?' – but generally he was involved in grimmer business and several times I noticed Mr Meek traipsing into the creative director's office and closing the door.

The old secretary Louise would cock her head at these movements but seemed more interested in the progress of a bout of flu through the firm. 'Mr Raikes's family had it over bank holiday,' she announced.

'Are you happy here?' asked Fanny during these troubled times.

'Are you?' I replied.

Fanny shook her head.

The gloom embraced the executives who visited our office – 'Hello, old thing,' said the man with the pigskin briefcase – and cast a shadow over meetings.

Getting up after one discussion, my head hit a low-slung lamp and a small cloud of dust, or dandruff, floated briefly in the bright light.

'Christ, ' I said.

In the lift each morning, there was further lugubriousness. One day, I stood next to my old boss Robin Peacock.

'New spectacles,' I remarked.

'Yes,' he replied.

In this atmosphere of mounting tension, Peter became increasingly guarded, tapping his office door shut whenever possible. From within would come the sound of his chair creaking, the rustle of paper bags, the click of a cigarette lighter, then furious typing followed by a sinister silence.

Sometimes I saw rapid movements through the frosted glass and gathered that Peter was cleaning his shoes.

When, at odd times of the day, he emerged, his face was set hard and his over-pressed American suit flapped past my desk without pausing. Some days, he had already put on his white padded mackintosh in order to make a quick getaway.

When later he bustled in again, the door would snap shut and I would immediately hear his voice on the telephone. If the door was left open one could see the flex of the telephone quivering as he listened to someone speaking. Sometimes a perfectly formed smoke ring floated into view.

Among Peter's visitors at this time was one of the account executive's secretaries, a girl named Chrissie.

One afternoon, I had seen them entering the building together after lunch. Now she was in the office, giving me a triumphant look as she sailed into Peter's private abode.

A few minutes later, the girl sailed off again, giving me another tart look. Peter then emerged and sauntered over to the job-seeking art director.

'Nice kid?' he asked in a low voice.

'Damn nice kid,' Roger replied.

My own affairs were of little interest to him. When I described an unexpected visit to the office from an out-of-work comedian I knew he simply declared, 'You're all hung up with these idiot people.'

Meanwhile, Peter's strange exits and entrances continued – sometimes inspiring more critical comments from others in the office. 'Ah, the Late Night Line Up! The Evening Show!' quipped one of the designers when Peter came in forty-five minutes late.

Some time passed before Peter revealed to me that he used these minor excursions to go gambling. In the little tourist casinos across the West End, he had enjoyed some success playing blackjack.

'I counted methodically. Like a bloody computer,' he said after winning a hundred pounds. Another day he returned looking black as thunder, sped past me as light-footed as a ballet dancer and when I opened the door of his office, seemed engaged in a ferocious search through his papers.

'I'm very, very irritated, almost bloody well leaving London tonight,' he fumed as he spread out various cheques and bills on his desk, in a manner which reminded me of my old colleague Toby.

Presently it emerged that he did not even have enough money for the gas meter at his flat and was reluctantly obliged to ask me for a small loan.

A few days later, the sacked art director slammed down his telephone and gave a great whoop of joy.

'I've got it!' he yelled. 'And the pubs are closed! Fuck 'em all! Redundant on June thirtieth! Bigger salary and head of television in a ten-million-pound agency July twentieth! This only happens in bloody fairy stories!'

The chorus of congratulations that this announcement provoked soon faded as rumours quickly circulated that other sackings were imminent.

'I know more about this than I'm prepared to say,' said one of the designers.

'Some of the things I know would astound you,' said Frank.

'Someone's head's going to roll,' said Fanny.

'It is dead interesting,' continued the designer.

I wondered when my own number would come up. In the lift one morning, Raikes eyed me unpleasantly and said, 'Continue with your work – never minding what the vicissitudes of fate may bring . . .' Another morning, he said, 'We might keep you on yet. My mind is ever-changing.'

The exact timing and reason for Peter's departure from the firm were not at all clear. Others were as mystified as myself.

'Is it true Pete's going back to the States?' asked a designer in dung-coloured trousers.

Then I heard Peter telephoning to someone far away, possibly in the south of France or Italy.

'I was thinking of coming down, Tom,' he shouted. 'How are you? In about nine days time. I'll talk to you on Friday, Tom.'

His legs were braced against the desk and the telephone flex was stretched out across the office. Suddenly, another perfect smoke ring floated through the doorway.

'All has turned out unexpectedly well on all fronts – books, friends, money,' he told me later. 'I'm not going to divulge any more to you. I'll pay you the money I owe you on Friday.'

For a while, everyone seemed to know more about Peter's situation than I did, but eventually he found time to tell me a few more details. 'All right with you?' he said grinning and showing his yellow teeth.

Further enquiries were met with, 'Mind your own business, William, thanks all the same,' and when I gingerly re-entered his office, he was talking on the telephone and flapped his hand dismissively.

Later the same day, Peter said more amiably, 'I'm just going to the bank. I'll meet you at the elevator.'

As the date of his departure drew nearer, Peter had various visitors to his office. Among these were Raikes, who said, 'That sounds much better. With your creative ability.'

To others, Raikes announced, 'We're losing one of our top writers, a really knock-out guy.'

Further effusiveness came from Mr Meek, ending with the lament, 'And horror of horrors, he's leaving us!'

From behind Peter's door I then heard the crackle of Sellotape being unrolled. He later emerged with a large brown paper parcel under his arm.

'You're looking well, William,' he said as he passed my desk.

For his last day in the office, Peter appeared in dark glasses.

'I'm just going to get a hot drink,' he said and went off and got a cup of chocolate which he came back holding with both hands.

'Pete's leaving today,' said one of the designers.

During the course of the day, various people called to wish him well.

'I hardly know you but I'd like to say goodbye to you,' said the executive with the pigskin briefcase.

Then Peter squeezed a tight roll of one-pound notes into my hands and asked in a low voice if his colleagues were doing a farewell presentation for him.

'I believe they are.'

'Oh shit.'

Finally, a large and elaborate card adorned with various signatures and messages was presented to him, amidst cries of 'Bye, Pete', 'See you, Pete' and 'Nice knowing you'.

A few moments after Peter had left the office for the last time, the telephone began to ring in his inner sanctum and a secretary rushed in to answer it. Commotion followed when the girl suddenly started screaming that he had left his farewell card behind on his desk.

'He didn't take his card,' she wailed.

There was pandemonium. 'He's only just this minute gone to the lift,' yelled one of the designers as people rushed to the windows. 'He can only just have got down there. Can I open this window? Is that him there?'

Peter had left his business files in immaculate order. 'I'll send you a letter,' were his last words to me, and a scrap of paper bearing the address, '13 via Carlucci' was the only clue as to his present whereabouts. Within hours, Fanny had moved triumphantly into the vacated office and her predecessor's once formidable reputation had been torn in shreds.

'I thought his copy was pretty indifferent.'

'He wasn't interested.'

'Was he sacked?'

'Of course he was.'

Others discussed Peter's supposed new life as a freelance script-writer.

'I think his wife's very decent to let him do it.'

'I think he was very cruel to women.'

'I'm sure there was something nice underneath, but I couldn't get through to it.'

Fanny's effervescence at her promotion did not last long. Soon I heard her remarking, out of the blue, 'Fed up!' Then came a protest about 'a cross-draught' in her new office – 'Has some idiot opened a window?' – and general displeasure with her own and other people's work.

When I presented her with an idea for a shampoo advertisement, she crumpled it up and dropped it into a waste-bin without a word.

Ugly rumours continued to intrude upon us. One afternoon I heard Frank entering Fanny's office saying, 'Before all hell breaks loose . . .' and closing the door behind him.

The next person to be sacked was Fanny herself.

Fanny took the news badly – her door slammed and I heard tears from within – but within hours she had rallied her forces, begun typing out job applications and dealing with other problems in her life.

'I'm extremely upset,' I heard her screaming on the telephone. 'I've never known anything like it in my life. This is true, actually. I only went to you because my other solicitors were so bad.'

During the next few days Fanny became more and more desperate and was caked in more and more make-up whenever she emerged from her office. Her quest for a new job soon proved successful, however, and there was general jubilation when she announced that she was moving to a rival firm where she would be working under a famous figure named Freddie Fry.

'You can't mention Raikes and Freddie Fry in the same breath,' said Fanny. 'Freddie Fry is a brilliant impresario.'

My own position remained uncertain. 'I'm just sitting here hoping the wind will blow in my favour,' I told Fanny as she made her farewells.

A few days later I was more than perplexed when Raikes swirled into the office and said, 'Well done, William, your job's saved. You were going to be chopped. Well done, have to go now. Hope you didn't mind my jokes all these weeks. Such a strong character.'

These words failed to reassure me. During the next few weeks, Raikes became uncannily obliging and agreeable but I was given less and less work. When I asked Frank if I could help him with his current tasks, he replied in the deadest of dead voices, 'If you want to . . .'

When I completed a piece of work and showed it to Frank for his approval, he replied in an equally joyless tone, 'Have to show it to Raikes these days.'

In the lift one morning, I had a further encounter with Robin Peacock.

After standing beside him in silence, I remarked, 'I can't think of anything funny to say.'

'Good,' he murmured. 'You've made my day.'

A more cheerful meeting took place one afternoon with my old boss Gordon. We met in the lift and trotted together across the reception area and into the street. He looked happy and well in high-heeled boots and purple-tinted spectacles and was smoking a cigarette through a long holder. Out on the pavement, buffeted – almost dancing – in the wind, he opened his briefcase, got out a new cigarette and snapped the case shut with one hand.

Suddenly he surprised me with fresh news of Toby.

Our old colleague, he said, had already left his job in
Brussels and was back in London looking for work.

'I'm afraid Toby is something of a drifter,' said Gordon
as he bundled himself into a taxi.

More inspiring news also came through about Peter.
He, too, was said to be back in London and had reputedly
had a novel accepted by a high-brow publisher. 'He told
me not to tell anyone at all,' said one of the designers still
attached to our group. A few days later, Peter's presence in
London seemed to be confirmed when I noticed the secretary
Chrissie sailing out of the building with a large wad of
typing paper under her arm.

In the middle of October, when I had been in the firm for
about twenty months, I was suddenly summoned to Mr
Meek's office along the corridor.

The tall administrator ushered me into his plant-filled
room and said, 'I always close the door when it's bad news.
And bad news it is.'

The news of my sacking spread quickly through the
creative department.

'My heart bleeds,' said Raikes.

Others took a more positive line. One of the designers
urged me to obtain the maximum redundancy payment –
and cited the old example of Sandy Scott.

'Sandy studied the legal niceties and got far more,' he
explained.   –

My remaining days in the firm were spent leaning
back at my desk and gazing at the ceiling.

One morning I arrived and found a new copywriter
installed beside me. He was a sloppy young man, whose

spine stuck out of his pullover when he leaned forward. He wore short socks and ochre-coloured slacks and was reading *The Times* in rather a sophisticated manner, turning the pages slowly and breathing heavily.

During our brief aquaintanceship, the newcomer addressed me as 'Dear boy' and boasted that he knew 'some of the whizz-kids at Warburg's'. Occasionally he snorted like an elephant and once I enraged him by picking a stray hair off his pullover and handing it to him politely.

On my last morning, I croaked goodbye to the creative director and answered various enquiries from my remaining colleagues about my future.

'Have you got anything lined up?'

'No.'

'Are you thinking of going to another shop?'

'No.'

'What will you be doing on Monday morning?'

'I don't know.'

June 1968

I WAS MUCH TOO EARLY for my appointment with Dr Freer. For twenty-five minutes I wandered around the area, crossing and recrossing the streets and occasionally pausing to peer at the brass name-plates beside each door. I was still too early when I eventually climbed the steps of the house in Harley Street, but the old, lame receptionist said, 'That's all right. Very wise. Make yourself comfortable. I'll fetch in the *Telegraph*.'

The carpet in the waiting-room had a homely pattern. On a central table were an unattractive plant and a book entitled *Great Events of the Royal Year 1953*. Through the window, I saw a van marked 'Medical and Surgical Equipment' making a delivery to the building opposite.

When the receptionist returned with the newspaper, she said, 'Dr Freer'll see you the moment he gets in.'

I had come across Dr Freer's name in an article in *The Times* and been struck by the photograph of his serious, determined-looking face. Tingling with nervousness I had telephoned his consulting room and been told by a rather jittery secretary to make my request for an appointment in writing. Dr Freer had then written saying he did not see patients without a letter from their general practitioner. 'Why do you want to see a psychiatrist?' asked the rosy-cheeked doctor whom I had so far only consulted about colds and other minor ailments but he had dashed off the necessary letter before I could reply.

A series of telephone calls to the nervy secretary followed. 'Are you there?' she asked after a long pause and then, 'Now look. Dr Freer's given me a letter offering you an appointment.'

At last I heard the glass-panelled front door crash shut and the sound of nimble footsteps hurrying down the hallway. A moment later the elderly receptionist appeared again – and directed me to a ground floor room at the back of the building.

Dr Freer was standing outside his consulting room, in the welcoming posture that a head waiter might assume at the entrance to a grand restaurant.

He was a sturdy, spruce man, with the build of a rugby player. His blond, greying hair was swept back without a parting. He was good-looking in a crude, slightly foreign way but seemed old for his age – which according to the Medical Register was only forty-two – and there was a sad, almost disillusioned look to his eyes. He wore a pale green check suit, a blue shirt and jazzy red tie.

The room into which he ushered me was half-curtained. There was a large desk in front of the window, a big low armchair and against the far wall a couch with a neat stack of cushions at one end.

Dr Freer closed the door and offered me the armchair. Then he sat down on a small upright seat at the desk, turned towards me and began his examination. He was business-like and methodical. His voice was nasal, slightly slurred and everything he said was delivered in a dry, haughty, worldly-wise manner. He said 'Years' instead of 'Yes', which suggested he was pondering over my replies. After a while, he put on a pair of large modern spectacles and began to jot down notes on a pad. At one junction he took off his spectacles and polished them with something from a drawer.

To begin with, Dr Freer seemed to be smiling quite a lot, keeping the conversation on a gentlemanly basis – 'Do you sleep well?' 'Yes, very well' – and when I told him I wanted to be a writer, he exclaimed cheerfully, 'Well, go and be a writer, then!' After a while, he seemed to have grown impatient, slapping his thigh and kicking his desk to get my attention.

I had approached the session with a pleasurable sense of anticipation, some amusement, even giggles – or was it nerves? – but now I was being reduced to pulp. Dr Freer's down-to-earth questions began to fall like hammer blows.

He asked me about my school-days, my attempt to go on the stage, my job in an advertising agency, my limited social life and friendships and finally my love life – or lack of it.

'There's nobody that you care for?'

'Not really.'

At one moment he suddenly removed his spectacles and leaned forward, staring at me really hard. Then, glancing quickly at the clock on his desk, he began to give his diagnosis in a sneering, fastidious voice. As he spoke, his lower lip began to descend, and he looked more and more like his photograph in the newspaper.

'If you think you're a comic genius, I think you're wildly mistaken,' he began.

'You need help,' he continued. 'You need to know yourself better. You're full of prejudices.'

'You think I've got prejudices?'

'Certainly, I think you've got prejudices. For one, you think you're a cut above everyone else. You're boastful. You seem to think you're some sort of rare bird. I think you're indulging in a large amount of defensive rationalization. I think if you really had a sense of humour, you'd be able to laugh at yourself more.'

I offered him a twisted smile of embarrassment.

'I don't think it's funny,' he shouted back at me. 'I think it's pathetic. I think you're a pathetic, lonely boy covering up terrible feelings of inadequacy and insecurity with delusions of grandeur – and I wish you'd stop it!'

Here he kicked his desk again in emphasis.

'If you don't agree with me, go and get a second opinion. There are plenty of other good psychiatrists in London.'

He delivered this last piece of advice with an angry shrug. Then he took up his pad again and scribbled another note. The meeting was over. Dr Freer seemed keen to get me out of the room. He stood up and turned towards the door. I was impressed by the immense broadness of his head and the way his hair grew into a furrow on his neck.

'Would you like to see yourself out?' he said.

He looked like a woodman who had just chopped down a tree.

A few days later, Dr Freer sent me a bill for six guineas and a letter suggesting that I might approach a certain Dr Drake for another opinion. I did so at once but Dr Drake wrote back saying he was far too busy to see anyone new and advised me instead to contact a certain Dr Jagger, who had an address in Devonshire Place.

Dr Jagger's secretary, to whom I soon spoke on the telephone, had a warm, open personality and seemed to create a lively and informal atmosphere round her employer. The first time I spoke to her she said chattily, 'Dr Jagger's at the Tavistock Clinic. Then he's got to pick up a patient.' When I rang her again the next afternoon, she said breezily, 'Dr Jagger's just gone out to buy a newspaper. Goodbye now!'

When Dr Jagger eventually came on the line, he twice called me 'Sir' and when I said I hoped my case could be dealt with in one session replied brightly, 'If it can be, it should be.'

The following week, I took a taxi to Devonshire Place and was ushered straight into Dr Jagger's consulting room. He was small and fat and wore an almost clownish double-breasted suit and an enormous orange tie which contrasted with the expanse of bright green carpet. He wore spectacles and had a helmet of thick curly hair. He handled our meeting with a fine, light touch. He offered me a cigarette and made mild mockery of psychological and psychiatric jargon.

'Extrovert, introvert,' he said, shrugging his shoulders. 'What does it matter?'

I said I was worried by the whiteness of my face but he assured me this was my natural complexion.

'Let's go back to square one', he said after a while. 'You're not suffering beyond what you can bear and you're doing no harm to anyone else.'

He concentrated instead on practicalities. If I was to become a writer, it was absolutely vital that I should have a literary agent.

'I know from bitter personal experience how essential it is,' he said, making a mournful expression.

He asked me what my income was and then said that I could not possibly afford psychoanalysis. Anyway, he was dubious about its advantages.

'It's long and expensive,' he said. 'You'd expect to learn a lot but might in fact learn very little.'

Such was the informality of the occasion that at the end of the session I asked Dr Jagger what I owed him.

'Eight guineas, please,' he said smartly.

As I wrote out a cheque for this amount, I asked Dr Jagger where he lived.

When he revealed that he owned a modern house near Hampstead Heath, I said rather crossly, 'Why do all psychiatrists have to live in Hampstead?'

Dr Jagger laughed and declared, 'I know what you're really angry about. Paying me eight guineas.'

'Brilliant,' I replied.

A few months later something caused me to consult my general practitioner again. I found that my file was already on his desk and he was reading a letter from it. I recognized Dr Freer's headed writing-paper but could not read much of the text of the letter which seemed to run to about fifteen lines.

'Just looking at the background,' said my doctor in a singsong voice.

I strained to see more of the letter and could make out

a few words and phrases: 'psychotic', 'the opposite sex' and 'delusions of grandeur' jumped off the page.

Then the doctor put the letter aside and asked what he could do for me.

I told him I had hurt my penis.

'Let me see it, please.'

After a fairly swift examination he declared that there was nothing in the least wrong with this part of my body. He then glanced sideways at Dr Freer's letter and made a clever remark.

'The problem is further up. In the head.'

June 1968–August 1969

THE FLAT WAS on the second floor of a block of studios. It was a calm, confident building – a few yards from the river – and consisted of three big studios with high, wide windows and three small ill-lit flats. Augustus John had lived here during the war and some time earlier James McNeill Whistler had – I think – occupied the top floor.

In the basement, a housekeeper lived with her husband. Her duties included cleaning the broad stone staircase and polishing the brass door-knockers. In the flat below me there lived a stout American lady, whose brightly coloured two-piece suits and matching hats and shoes did not belong in this corner of Chelsea. In the studio across the staircase was a portrait painter called Tom, who had a stubbly beard and twinkling eye. The most celebrated inhabitant of the building was the young tailor who lived and worked downstairs. Mr Magic was his name and his customers included the Rolling Stones and other contemporary figures.

I had a job in advertising – I will not bore you with the details – and left the building early each morning and returned well after six often too exhausted to do anything other than sprawl on my single bed and listen to the sounds of laughter and merriment getting louder and louder in the flats across the street.

My own social life was practically non-existent. My only friend at this time was called Peter. He worked in the same firm and had written a novel for which he had not yet found a publisher. Even he was often reluctant to visit me – 'Pay my taxi fares both ways?' he asked when I begged him to come over. At other times he called uninvited, bustling into the flat saying, 'Caught you with your pants down!' or something equally combative.

Eventually we would relax together and he might say, 'You're all nerves anywhere outside your apartment,' or make some other double-edged gesture of intimacy. 'You are my only friend,' he said one evening, then qualified this assertion by adding, 'I can only get on with sick people – I don't mean crazy.'

On one visit, he used my telephone to call his girlfriend who worked in a bank. 'Hello, what are you doing?' I heard him ask. 'Nothing, I'm round at William's. Howdya feel? Yah, I feel terrible too.'

Such interludes were brief. Many of my evenings were spent lolling about alone, listening to the sweep of traffic on the Embankment and the low boom of river barges – or staring out of the window. Sooner or later, I would move to the big mirror above the fireplace and start staring at myself in various poses – sometimes clowning, sometimes frowning, sometimes adopting the lugubrious features of the psychiatrist with whom I had recently spent an inconclusive hour in Harley Street.

At weekends, I rallied myself, bought old Persian rugs from a local dealer – 'You are a clever boy. I like to help young people. Your mother and father will be pleased with you' – and made other attempts to brighten up my surroundings.

I also began to use these idle hours to start writing – and after a few weeks invited my colleague Peter to come around and read my first tentative scribblings.

'Jesus,' he said after a few moments. 'It's really fantastic. This'll win you thousands of readers, plus sales. Jesus, it's really interesting.' With a coffee mug balanced on the arm of his chair, he turned the pages of my scrappy manuscript. 'Sshhh, wait on,' he said.

'Bored?' I asked.

'No, it's really terrific.'

He scratched his head excitedly, then his armpit. A few moments later, he tweaked his ginger sideburn and made a noise like a racing car rounding a tricky bend.

'Oh, shit,' he yawned. 'Not so good. Terribly boring. Oh, Jesus, it's bloody boring. Very old-fashioned.'

'Any advice you can give me?'

'Naah,' he said. 'You're writing it.'

After a few moments' silence, Peter announced, 'Back to my problems now.'

'Are you all right?' the American lady on the floor below occasionally asked me. I was slowly getting to know the building and its inhabitants better. One evening, I watched the tailor unpacking his car. He did so slowly and gently, crossing the road carrying small, neatly wrapped parcels. His pale face, long pointed nose and wispy figure were enhanced by a little leather jerkin and tight tweed trousers. When we met in the doorway he said nothing but gave me a soft, easy grin to which I responded with a shy smile of my own. The painter Tom was more robust. He looked like Father Christmas and his presence in the building had a festive effect. I was reassured by his proximity, his hum on the stairs and the smell of cigars and oil paint that issued from his studio. One Saturday morning I heard him complimenting the housekeeper Mrs Angel – 'I say!' – on the newly cleaned staircase windows. Another afternoon I heard him opening his door to an unexpected guest – 'Christ! Come in!' – and later at night there were sometimes softer footsteps on the stairs and I would hear Tom welcoming a visitor with much more affectionate tones.

Peter's visits to my flat were infrequent – and our discussions revolved monotonously around my aspirations to be a writer. 'You're procrastinating,' he said on one occasion. 'Get down to it.' A few weeks later he read more of my stuff, and pronounced, 'You've found your form,' and added cheerily, 'Polishing up is the most pleasurable bit.'

Our relationship remained volatile, however, and I was not altogether surprised when at the end of that summer Peter left the advertising agency, and then the country, without fully explaining the circumstances. The acceptance of his novel by a highbrow publisher played some part in this turn of events but Peter did not go into details. His last words to me were, 'I'll write you a letter.'

A few weeks later, I was made redundant myself and thereafter spent even more time sitting in the second-floor flat, staring at the old gas fire and the cool cream cavern in which it was enclosed, wandering from room to room, waiting for the post or gazing out of the window.

The back of the flat looked through a fine tracery of leaves on to the dome, towers and chimneys of the Royal Hospital. During the day, bursts of infantry music came from this direction, and at night the view was adorned by a luminous blue clock at least a mile off. From the front room, I could observe the activities on the pavement below. The street was a backwater yet full of incident. Front doors were forever opening and slamming shut, door-knockers rattled, workmen whistled and cleaning ladies clattered dustbin lids. Then came more colourful events: mounted police cantered down the street, police sirens wailed and a famous photographer zoomed up in an Aston Martin to see Mr Magic.

I had realized some time ago that the tailor downstairs was at the centre of a select group of young people, white-faced musicians and their friends, who spoke in fey voices and wore the close-fitting velvet suits and frilly shirts that Mr Magic had helped make fashionable. They arrived on the backs of motorbikes or crammed into limousines – on one occasion holding up a lorry delivering central-heating oil to the flats opposite – and were always made welcome. 'Have you come to see us?' asked the tailor when strangers arrived for his services and attentions.

From my front window, I also had an excellent view of the large dilapidated mansion down the street where for many months I had been a lodger. From time to time, I heard the slam of its grand front door and saw familiar and unfamiliar people, and sometimes my imposing old land-lady, spilling out onto the street.

Other sounds came from the block of flats immediately opposite. One day I heard a trumpet being played extremely badly. Another time, a slapping noise from an empty room indicated the presence of a builder or decorator. Listening carefully, I might hear a telephone ringing deep inside the building and from an upper floor there often echoed a shrill exchange of voices which could have come straight off a West End stage.

Down on the street, I occasionally met my neighbours and their visitors in the flesh. I was often lost for words.

'How's your dog?' I asked an old man.

'The same,' he replied.

The tiny housekeeper at the block opposite was more talkative. One day she informed me she was cooking a steak pudding. The recipe, she said, required a full bottle of red wine, half a pound of mushrooms and a host of other ingredients. 'Steam it for seven hours,' she shouted after me.

From time to time, I also addressed chauffeurs bringing clients to Mr Magic.

'Whose is this car?' I asked the man in charge of a blue Rolls-Royce.

'It's Freddie Fry's, the advertising man.'

'I saw a very young person in it the other day.'

'That's him.'

'How old is he?'

'Twenty-five.'

Winter came. Sometimes I got up early and walked the streets in my somewhat dirty camel-hair coat. Other days I remained in my ill-made bed, overawed by the mist which rendered the block opposite only dimly visible and subdued even the sounds of the birds. Other mornings I was woken by shafts of sunshine and harsher noises, dustmen devouring the street or the whistle of the postman on his rounds.

I had already begun to attach importance to the post and place hopes on what it might bring though there was no particular news I was waiting for. Every morning I listened for the postman's whistle and the sound soon became so familiar that I did not need to check upon his approach from the window. Then came a delay while he stood pushing material through the letter-box or chatting with Mrs Angel downstairs.

I discovered I was not the only person in the building waiting for the post. Many mornings, the tailor's charlady stood competitively poised at his ground-floor door, looking at her watch and fingernails as she waited to seize Mr Magic's mail. It was under her gaze that I sometimes opened the letter-box and found nothing – or glanced stupidly into my empty pigeon-hole if someone else had already sorted the incoming letters.

One morning, my descent of the staircase was delayed by the sound of whispers between the tailor's charlady and Mrs Angel but when I eventually reached the lobby, I was delighted to find a letter from Peter.

The letter came from Santo Domingo – wherever that was – and was followed a few weeks later by a picture postcard from Naples showing an all-male gypsy dancing troupe, on which Peter had merely scrawled, 'It's the quick steps that throw you.'

Early in the New Year, my old colleague was back in England. He had driven himself from Italy in a saucy red sports car and brought with him a whiff of international life peopled by exotic individuals with exciting names. 'Ginger Baker was on the boat coming over,' he told me. 'Bright red hair and a dead white face. He was in a two-tone Jensen with two girls. Very impressive.'

Peter had come to London to see his publishers. I was in awe of these developments but he assured me that I, too, was making progress at last. 'It's good you're not working. That's the way to get ahead. Whatever happens, you'll be better off.'

Within hours of his arrival, he had become immersed in my domestic life, requesting tomatoes on toast, snapping up the offer of an orange and providing a running commentary on his health. 'I usually wear these glasses in the morning because my eyes are tired,' was followed by, 'I can always tell I'm tired by an aching in my thighs.'

He also responded keenly to my suggestion that he should rent a room in the big house up the street where I had been a lodger. 'Call her up, make an appointment,' he said and with surprising ease had secured the room that had once been mine.

By the evening, he was sufficiently installed there to decline my suggestion that we had supper together. 'I think I'll try and catch up with some correspondence,' he said.

During the days that followed, from my second-floor window I observed Peter's stealthy, darting exits and entrances. It soon emerged that he had learned the ways of the old house – 'You get the feeling that people are listening' – and formed a particular affection for the odd-jobman who worked there. 'I saw him this morning, bringing in the milk,' he told me one day. 'He was wearing a brown cap and mittens. He looked very good.'

He had also formed an admiration for my old landlady. Mrs Drinkwater, he said, was so different to the 'sticky-beaks' he had known in the past. One day she had rapped on his door – 'very self-possessed, very secure' – and one afternoon he had visited the old lady in her own quarters. 'She was thumbing through an old photograph album,' he reported. 'She doesn't smile straight away. She doesn't make some stupid little laugh or apologize.'

The purpose of this visit to Mrs Drinkwater was to ask if he could share his room with his new girlfriend, who was shortly due to arrive from Italy.

The request had been granted without fuss. At the end of January, Peter's girlfriend arrived in England and moved in across the street. She was cool and commanding in a withdrawn sort of way, taller than Peter but closely knit with him. When I saw them returning together from King's Road carrying parcels of food, they looked like a busy, happy little unit and when I beckoned at my old colleague from my window, he scowled up and said, 'I'm terribly busy' and 'No, I don't want to come up.'

Life on my side of the street began most days with the reassuring sound of coughing from Tom's studio followed by the slam of his door as he set out for breakfast. I listened to his descending footsteps and then the buzz of his car going up the street. He would return more slowly, getting out of his car with a cigar quivering in his mouth and sometimes a bottle of whisky in his hand. He entered the building with an air of leisure and enthusiasm I envied, happy though alone, climbing the stairs and re-entering his studio whistling.

Tom's flow of sitters continued and once or twice a week I heard unfamiliar footsteps as some Captain of Industry trudged upstairs to have his portrait painted, while down on the street the visitor's chauffeur quickly got out, and into, a pack of home-made sandwiches.

At the beginning of February, a new figure moved into our block. For some weeks I had noticed the arrival of letters and invoices addressed to a Miss Sally Walker and then learned that the vacant studio above me had been let to someone of this name, though she herself had not yet moved in.

One afternoon, I heard the arrival of a powerful shooting-brake and met my new neighbour on the staircase. She was a tall girl, imposingly adult and expensively dressed in a fur coat, velvet trouser suit and long leather boots. She was a dog-painter by profession and the owner of two animals herself, a saluki and a long-haired dachshund.

Sounds from upstairs told me that the newcomer had begun arranging the large room to her liking and soon a note appeared downstairs saying, 'Two pints of Jersey milk please'. A few days later, these impressions of a well-organized life were confirmed when Miss Walker invited me to tea, offering hot buttered toast and Gentleman's Relish beside her studio gas fire, while she cosseted the smaller of her two pets. 'Pat-a-Cake got fleas and I had to wash her,' she crooned, and when I over-praised this little dog she said, 'Pat-a-Cake, d'you hear what he's sayin' about you?'

During the weeks that followed, I grew accustomed to the tap of the newcomer's heels as she sauntered across the floor above, followed by the pitter-patter of clawed feet.

With the aid of photographs, Sally was working calmly towards an exhibition later in the year. None of her creature comforts or domestic routines would be suspended. Each morning I heard her float downstairs to collect her newspaper and milk – or to see to the post. As a neighbourly gesture she would sometimes leave a friendly message for me outside my door and in the afternoon she might include me in her fireside tea or invite me to watch the 'telly' that she had hired. I quickly got used to the welcome from the dogs and sometimes even dared to ask, 'Will there be tea today?' When she was out, I missed her – I was consoled by the barks and howls of the dogs left upstairs – and when she told me she was leaving London earlier than planned, I felt lost. From my window, I watched the two dogs prancing and darting about as their luxuriously clad mistress placed various objects in the back of her badly parked car and occasionally shouted their names in exaggerated reproof.

My dealings with my neighbour Tom went through ups and downs. One night I was alarmed to hear him stumbling upstairs – followed by the uncharacteristic crash of his studio door closing. When I met him on the staircase the following morning he immediately asked me to have a drink with him at a local club, but when I tried to return his hospitality a few days later, he declined with the words, 'I can't. I'm terribly sorry. I'm off in two minutes.'

My relationship with Peter had also become increasingly tricky. Visiting my flat one evening he told me I was 'too way-out' and was even moved to criticize my surroundings: 'When are you going to clean this dump?' My literary efforts no longer interested him and he brushed aside my further attempts at writing by saying, 'It's money in the bank, that one.'

One night I asked him over and he responded, 'Can't you bear the loneliness?' And when I asked him something about his novel's publication date, he replied, 'Don't ask stupid questions, William.'

One day, Peter and his girlfriend drove me to Sloane Square station but did so with bad grace. After dropping me off, Peter rapped out, 'Call me when you turn twenty-one,' and I feebly replied, 'Okay.'

A few days later, normal relations were restored. Over coffee in my flat, Peter pronounced, 'Baudelaire had a horror of being easily understood,' and then complimented me on the aftershave lotion I was wearing. 'It's terrific,' he said. 'How much does it cost?' He also enquired about others in my building: 'Where's Sally Walker now? When's Sally Walker coming back?'

One evening, he broke into my solitude by bringing round his editor at the publisher's, a small girl with blonde curls, and having made this informal introduction he suggested I telephone her – 'I think she's depressed,' he said.

The following day, he asked, 'Listen, er, have you rung Stella?' and later seemed disgruntled when I refused to describe the evening that she and I spent together.

Soon after this little episode, he asked, 'Do you have any big secrets I don't know about?' and one night I returned to find a note pinned on my doorbell, saying, 'Where the hell are you at 12.30 a.m.?'

After this brief revival of interest, the coolness resumed

and the red sports car parked outside the house up the
street became a constant reminder of the bungled friendship. Sometimes its door was open when I passed by.
Sometimes Peter was at the wheel, leaning forward with a
fixed smile on his face. Sometimes I saw Peter and his
girlfriend walking arm-in-arm on the Embankment and
took steps to avoid them.

In the middle of March, Peter suddenly disposed of
his car. A few days later, I returned from a visit to the
doctor to find a further note for me saying, 'Tomorrow, I
take an early flight to Los Angeles. I'll see you at a
subsequent juncture in the voyage.'

The next morning I looked out of my window at an
early hour and saw Peter's trim figure moving deftly
between the parked cars. He carried suitcases and other
personal effects to a waiting taxi.

I was left to labour over my writing and wait for the
post. I had now begun to submit things to publishers, and
was thus even more fixated on the twice-daily visits of the
postman. Around eight each morning I began listening for
his whistle. Then I became glued to the building, refusing
to go out for fear of missing a delivery of mail. Some
mornings I would foolishly nip downstairs three times in
succession and still find empty pigeon-holes and nothing in
the box either. I watched the postman's movements with
keener and keener interest and even learned to recognize his
reflection in a window opposite. His perambulations
puzzled me. One day I saw him entering the block opposite
and not appearing for five minutes. Another day I saw him
returning from the river end of the street with an empty
sack yet there was still no post downstairs.

Such anticipation was futile but bad news was better than none and I even became excited by the sound of the postman struggling to push my rejected manuscripts through the ground-floor letter-box.

Later in the day, other sounds diverted me: a swishing noise as a motor-bike messenger mounted the staircase in a waterproof garment, or the arrival of new sitters for Tom.

One of these was a famous old author. I passed this venerable figure on the staircase and noticed he was wearing the same hat and mackintosh he had worn in a television documentary. I heard Tom opening his door and the visitor apologizing for being early: 'I got a lift in a tradesman's van.' Tom said, 'All right?' and closed the door quickly.

Further encounters took place in the downstairs lobby. One day, Mr Magic and a girl were struggling together to control a large puppy. 'Down! Down!' said the tailor when the creature sprang up at me. 'Leave him alone!' shouted his companion.

On the same spot I had occasional brushes with the stout American lady who lived in the flat below me. Sometimes I saw her returning by taxi, with a neat wad of newspapers under her arm, and one morning she asked me sharply if I still had no job. When I replied with a firm negative, she continued, 'So you're still a man of leisure then? How do you manage it?'

Fear of such embroilments drove me on to the streets – and sometimes as far as the West End – though the start of these excursions was likely to be a further encounter on the street.

One day I passed the house where I had been a lodger

and found the door half-open and my old landlady Mrs Drinkwater slowly emerging with the aid of her walking-sticks.

'I'm terribly lame and tired,' she began apologetically.

The spring brought bad weather. Wind and rain lashed the tree at the back of the house and rattled the flap of an air-vent in a nearby building. Water dropped from the eaves and down the chimney into the fireplace. Cars passed below with a familiar swish – and from my window I saw the tailor, his hair now as long as a girl's, hurrying into the building.

I continued to write – but now learned that the tap-tap of my typewriter and my movements about the flat as I attempted to drum up inspiration were disturbing to the American lady below. One day she complained that she had heard me going 'up and down, up and down'.

I, too, had to contend with unwelcome sounds. Not the least of these was the slap of wings as pigeon after pigeon swept up and landed on a ledge above my window. Then would come a grumbling noise from inside a cavity a few feet above my head which persuaded me to consult the housekeeper Mrs Angel about the problem.

A few days later, I sat flinching at my desk while a long ladder was propped against the outer wall of the building. The sound of a man – then men – climbing its rungs was followed by voices: 'It's an odd shape', 'You can't get in there' and 'It goes down at the back.'

A few days later, the pigeons reappeared on the window-sill and the feverish murmurings within the wall were renewed.

These distractions were soon combined with louder noises from above. The studio upstairs had now been let to a fashion model with a dynamic life. In person, the new tenant seemed cool, poised and immaculate but everything else about her life seemed chaotic. Night after night, I heard her tearing to and fro across the ceiling, her footsteps unnecessarily hurried as she lunged about in ungainly movements. Sometimes she kept a taxi waiting downstairs as she stormed around changing her clothes. Then came the clatter of high heels descending the stone staircase and at last the soothing sound of the taxi rattling away up the street.

One night the usual indications of panic and turmoil above me were replaced by an urgent battering sound. The following day, the new tenant explained to me that she had taken a sleeping pill and forgotten that her mother was coming round. 'She was in a terrible tizz. You may have heard her banging on the door. She was beginning to imagine the worst had happened. She's completely dependent on me, you see.'

After several months of silence, letters and cards had begun to arrive again from Peter. He was still in America but stated that he would soon be in England again. A telephone call followed in which he told me, in an unfamiliar coarse accent, that he would be arriving the following Thursday. I suggested that he stayed with me for a few days. A telegram then proclaimed his precise time of arrival.

I was excited to see my old colleague but realized almost immediately that he was in low spirits. His novel had been published but entirely ignored by the critics. His future plans were unclear.

The flat displeased him more than before. 'What stinks here?' he asked after his first night under my roof, and then answered his own question. 'The trash!' he exclaimed.

The neighbours also offended him – 'Is that hair really necessary?' he asked of Mr Magic's new coiffeur – and his mind seemed fixed on Los Angeles where his girlfriend remained. Several times a day, telephone calls came from this direction and whenever I was out or asleep he attempted to return these messages. Such was his desperation on this account that at one moment he pressed some money on me and suggested I go out and buy food. I obligingly did so but returned sooner than expected and heard the telephone click down the moment I turned my key in the mortise. Peter was embarrassed and told me he had been talking to the Speaking Clock.

After this unnerving incident, I started leaving my telephone off the hook but this did not prevent Peter trying to use the extension and swearing when it refused to function. 'Jesus Christ,' I heard him muttering at the other end of the line.

I realized that Peter had returned to England in order to try and get a job in advertising again.

He had turned his back on this trade some time ago but was now hurriedly trying to make up some samples to show prospective employers.

'D'you know a good typewriter repair shop?' he called from the other room. Later, there were cries of 'Oh, shit!' and 'Have you got an eraser?' When I said, 'No', he said, 'You're kidding?' Then came, 'You must have more magazines than this. Jesus, these scissors are terrible. What are you smoking that stupid cigar for?'

These bouts of furious activity were followed by calmer times. 'I'll just go and fling myself on my bed,' he said one evening, but the tension between us continued to build up and I noted that Peter's disappointment over his novel and disgust with the contemporary literary scene had spread to the entire British tradition.

'Name me one great British writer of the nineteenth century,' he suddenly challenged me.

'Emily Brontë,' I responded.

'Bullshit,' he replied.

Things came to a peak when a letter arrived informing me that a magazine had at last accepted something I had written. Peter had long ago lost interest in my scribblings – 'Type it up. Send it off,' was all the advice he had offered me lately.

'Really good news,' I said entering the flat with the letter of acceptance in my hand.

'Where's the cheque? Where's the cheque?' asked Peter.

A few hours later, he added, 'You're going to be a success, William.'

Things were still turbulent when, after ten days together, Peter suddenly left the flat – his destination undisclosed. During our last breakfast, he asked, 'What can we put on the toast? Jesus Christ, don't you have any jam? What's so funny?'

Without the diversion of Peter's presence, I lapsed into the solitary practices of the past. Sometimes I lit a cigarette and watched myself smoking it, noticed that my lips were cracked and that there was blood on the fag end. Sometimes I carefully examined a fly that lay spread-eagled on my cuff or stared back at the pigeon on the window-ledge. Sometimes, these encounters stirred me into action. One evening, ten or twelve flies whizzing silently and pointlessly around the centre of the room annoyed me enough to swat the lot. Another day, I rescued a wasp from a honey pot and watched it cleaning itself and eventually fly out of the window.

One afternoon, these reveries were interrupted by the arrival of a man from another carpet shop.

'What a pity! What a pity!' he said as he looked at the emaciated specimens I had bought a year earlier and was now anxious to sell. Then he added, 'You might get someone stupid enough to pay ten pounds for the pink one.'

Another afternoon, I was surprised by a visit from an out-of-work comedian I had not seen for many months. He swung into the flat and greeted me effusively, accepted a mug of coffee but declined more substantial refreshment.

'No thank you. I'm not hungry,' he said. 'How are you anyway? Ah, good.'

Noticing the big mirror above the fireplace, he then declared, 'It's like a night-club here, isn't it?'

Later we walked together through the streets. 'You love Chelsea, don't you?' he remarked. 'It's like a village, isn't it?'

With my neighbour Tom I had more regular encounters. One day he knocked on my door asking if he could borrow a bow-tie. 'Thanks awfully,' he said as I handed him the item I had as yet found very little use for.

Ten minutes later, I watched my dinner-jacketed neighbour's car circling in the road and speeding off up the street.

I was back at the window the following day when a horse and dray arrived to deliver plants for Mr Magic's garden. Then the tiny housekeeper from the flats opposite called up at me from across the street.

'You're looking very white! When are you going to clean your windows?' Then she pointed at a cat limping behind her. 'Always following me!'

Whenever we met on the street, the old lady filled me in on her pet's latest problems.

'Ginger's crippled,' she told me. 'His legs don't go out properly at the back.'

Another day she said, 'Ginger got stung by a bumble bee in his ear. I had to bathe it.'

She also talked of the dramas in her block, how she had knocked over a bottle of ink in someone's flat. 'I got drowned,' she said and added defiantly that the tenant concerned was 'an old crab'.

I took various walks. Mist drew me to the river and I took a few paces beside this arm of the sea from which came the hoot of old-fashioned tugboats. Sunshine drew me to King's Road, where I began walking with a certain high spirits, as if I were on the deck of a luxury ship. Outside a café, I found Tom sitting comfortably, puffing at a cigar. Further along, I shrank from someone I'd worked with in the advertising agency, a portly individual, who was bundling himself into a funny old sports car. In Sloane Square itself, I spotted the housekeeper Mrs Angel and her husband going full-tilt through the crowds but in opposite directions.

Returning from this jaunt, I called at the grocery store on the corner of my street. The man behind the counter was on the telephone – 'All right, Mrs Drinkwater,' he said. 'Right. Right. Sometime today then.'

A heat wave came at last. Sun blanched the street and gave the old mansion where I had once lodged a continental look. A racing commentary droned on in one of the flats opposite. Children ran down the pavement blowing squeakers and hooters. In the back garden, Mr Magic gave tea parties for his friends. The leisurely chitchat which filtered up the wall – plus the scrape of a china cup – contrasted starkly with the noise from the street of metal bolts being hurled into the back of a lorry.

One afternoon, I leafed through an evening newspaper and learned that the temperature that day had already touched 'a sizzling 105 on Putney Hill' – while an item on another page informed me that my neighbour Mr Magic was to marry the girl with the unruly dog.

That night, there were further celebrations in the garden below me. Other people arrived later and the tree I admired was bathed in light till three in the morning.

Early the following Friday, I watched the tailor, now wearing patched jeans, loading his car with unhurried movements and looking carefully to the left and right each time he crossed the road.

Later that day, noisier neighbours wished each other 'Goodbye' and 'Have a nice journey up' as well as checking up on their directions. 'You branch off before Newmarket, don't you?'

The next day, the street was dead with no sounds from above or below until an aeroplane suddenly roared across the hazy blue sky. Then came the sound of a boy kicking a can down the pavement. At the end of the day all peace was shattered by a burglar alarm going off and persisting into the night.

One Sunday, my old landlady Mrs Drinkwater recruited me to push her smart new wheelchair to a church three streets away.

'Oh, the Ninetieth Psalm!' she exclaimed as we slowly entered the building together.

'Yes, I'm afraid you've missed that,' said a verger.

An hour later, I pushed the old lady home and after heaving herself into her house, she proclaimed that I would be rewarded for my kindness with 'pillows in heaven'.

Inside my own building, all was quiet. Tom was away and so was the fat American lady downstairs. The tailor and his friends were dispersed across England or further afield. Only the housekeeper and her husband remained on the premises and my occasional encounters with them were discomfiting.

One morning, I opened the door of my flat unaware that Mrs Angel was in the process of polishing its brass knocker. The housekeeper had fallen back against the wall of the staircase, white with shock.

Another morning, I was interrupted while lolling in my bath by an angry telephone call from Mr Angel to say that I was activating the overflow.

Most nights, I sat listening to the cars swooping along

the Embankment or lay in bed, the ball of one foot locked on to the knee-cap of the other leg, brooding about the past and future. From time to time I pulled myself together and launched into some time-wasting diversion.

One afternoon, I telephoned a film production company with a very particular purpose in mind.

'Such a funny man on the line,' I heard the operator tell her colleague. 'Wants the script of *Marnie*.'

January 1965–March 1966

I HAD LEFT SCHOOL with one idea in my head. I wanted to be a professional comedian. The various vague visions of my life as a Man of Letters which had sustained me during adolescence had been suddenly replaced by one fanatical idea. I wanted to be a solo variety artist, a stand-up comic, clowning, telling jokes, making a fool of myself in front of large audiences. I had no other interests on any level.

Within weeks of leaving school I had obtained interviews with several of the big theatrical agencies in London, though I had not yet worked out what form my 'act' should take. These firms had been happy to see me and I had been spellbound by their offices, the posters for past and current shows in their corridors and waiting-rooms and all the hard-nosed atmosphere of theatrical management – but after a while they had grown impatient with me and my requests for work. 'Go to Manchester!' a man at the Bernard Delfont office had suddenly bellowed at me. 'Go to Manchester! There's tons of work up there!'

A few days later, I had taken the train north in a sort of dream. Ten miles out of Euston, I had passed the jagged silhouette of my old boarding school with only the briefest sideways glance. My aspirations to become a comedian had

been a well-kept secret there and if I had had any reputation
at all among my school-fellows it was for a certain solem-
nity. A hundred or so miles later I crossed the Trent–Mersey
canal with mounting excitement. The enormous built-up
area I was entering, the blackened banks of the railway line,
the filthy allotments and old brick chimneys puffing smoke
in every direction, both thrilled and intimidated me. I
knew little of this world except that it seemed to stretch
from Coventry to Liverpool, from Liverpool to Leeds,
forming a conurbation far larger than the London area.
Bleak and unfamiliar though it was, I felt I was entering a
land of infinite promise. As far as I was concerned, the
industrial might of the nineteenth century had generated a
cabaret audience of unlimited size.

On arrival in Manchester, I stepped off the train with
a light step, entered the nearest telephone kiosk and dialled
a number. A man with a soft, girlish voice had quickly
offered me a week's work at a pub called The Man In The
Moon. I then strutted excitedly about the city. The cobbled
streets seemed full of people with theatrical connections.
The men wore artificial fur jackets, jazzy bow-ties, natty
slacks, funny hats – clothing which I thought peculiar to
the entertainment profession. Their bushy, prematurely
grey hair made them all look like showmen – and the
colourfully dressed and coiffeured women with them could
have easily been singers, dancers or at least theatrical
landladies. On every corner there seemed to be some pub,
club, casino or working men's institute offering 'a host and
compère' and 'a resident duo' if not 'star cabaret', while on
many office doorways I found a name-plate revealing that

some showbiz organization – 'Ted Cod Enterprises', 'Phil Tumney Entertainments' – was located within.

The theatricality was pervasive. Even in the pubs where there was no official cabaret, men would stand up and tell a dirty joke, big women would do an impromptu high kick and peculiar parlour tricks would be performed. When the pubs closed, music began to issue from the basements of the disused factory buildings and warehouses which filled the centre of the city. From murky premises with names such as 'The Stardust Room', 'The Paradise Club' and the 'El Morocco' there came the gurgle of a saxophone and the throb of an electric organ, followed by the bark of a comedian's patter.

On the night of my unexpected dismissal by The Man In The Moon, I returned to the city centre looking for something to eat. I found a café near a railway station. A rowdy party burst out laughing as I entered. A waitress said, 'Yes, luv?' and I sat down as far away as possible from the others.

Ten minutes later, a man in an apron appeared and said, 'Have you ordered?'

Eventually I was eating a Spanish omelette to the accompaniment of further cackles from the other side of the café. Finally one of the revellers eyed what I was eating and spoke directly to me.

'Have you put your girlfriend in that?'

My inability to get laughs from a paying audience did not deflect me from my purpose or shatter my deeply rooted image of myself or prevent me getting further involved in show business. By the end of the week, I had appeared on

stage twice more. First an unpaid audition at a large
working men's club in a suburb called Eccles; then, later
the same night, a paid appearance in a small basement club
in the city centre. At the working men's club, the master
of ceremonies at first refused to allow me to appear – 'I
can't put you on out there. They'd crucify you' – and,
indeed, I got no reaction at all from the audience of
unsmiling men and their wives. My appearance in the little
nightclub, where there were only about ten people present,
went better, and when I forgot my words and had to
produce a list of jokes, there were a few loud laughs.

The next day, I moved into a hostel near the biggest
station. It offered two grades of room. I chose a nineteen-
and-sixpenny one without wash-basin and looking on to the
inner well of the building. The lady in the kiosk opened a
little tin to find some change and said, 'Tut-tut.'

Then I telephoned the agent who had given me my
first booking. He immediately whispered, 'I hear you died
the death in Eccles, William.'

So began my life as a stand-up comic. During the next
few weeks I made dozens of paid and unpaid appearances in
Manchester's pubs and clubs. Managers and compères were
often reluctant to put me on. 'All right, William, let's see
what you're made of,' they would say grudgingly. Sometimes pennies were thrown on to the stage. Sometimes I
got the slow handclap. Frequently I was 'paid off' – given
half the agreed fee and told not to return. After each show
I would make my way back to the hostel, ring an outside
doorbell as it was usually long after midnight, and then
climb a staircase to the third floor. My nights there were
not comfortable. I was moved from room to room. More

than once I slept in someone's dirty sheets. Most nights the central-heating system rattled and banged, and other residents chattered long into the small hours making me scream out in protest from my bed. In the morning I would wash my socks and underpants in the communal sink and leave them to dry on my sooty window-sill – and then sometimes forgot them, producing high-pitched cackles from the team of ladies who arrived to make the beds.

Each morning, I would rebook a room and go out on to the streets. Each day, I would wander from library to snack-bar, from station to hotel. 'Ta, luv,' from a waitress were sometimes the only words spoken to me for hours on end.

A great deal of my time was spent in the imposing old-fashioned hotel where I had first stayed on arrival in the city.

It was from here that I telephoned the clubs and agents to arrange my bookings – and it was here that I licked my wounds after disastrous nights. In the gents' lavatory at this hotel I picked up two fragments of soap and rubbed them together to make lather. The attendant laughed and said this practice betrayed that I came from the south of England.

Many of my appearances took place in the small hours, which meant sitting up either in the big hotel or in my room at the hostel waiting for midnight, attending to my personal appearance and rehearsing my act with the aid of a heart-shaped hand-mirror.

On stage I wore a pin-striped suit or a loud check jacket and I slicked back my hair with Brylcreem. Instead of wearing make-up, I stained my face with a sun-tan lotion which had to be renewed every couple of days and smelled rather unpleasant. The glory of my wardrobe was the new camel-hair coat I had bought in London before Christmas. Thick and luxurious, it lent me a certain authority when I called at an agent's office or arrived at a club to do my act.

Dressed in this garment, I could override doormen's requests for 'Ten shillings, sir' with a haughty 'I am an artiste' and even compères and musicians were fooled into treating me as if I were some sort of professional.

'There's one spot at ten-thirty,' I would be told. 'And one at twelve.'

All illusions must have vanished once I stepped on stage. I was usually introduced with a burst of loud music, a slow march. Sometimes I fell over before I reached the microphone – a piece of clowning that caused alarm rather than amusement. I would begin by singing a popular song out of tune – and the hesitantly delivered patter that followed did not, could not, save the situation. I usually forgot my lines and had to fumble in my pocket for a list of jokes. Sooner or later, I would be talking to myself. Members of the audience would drift past the bandstand where I stood alone, without props. If I was not booed off, I would end my act with another piece of tuneless song and then skip off the stage, blowing kisses and shouting against the non-existent applause, 'God bless you! Goodnight everybody!'

My act worried my fellow artistes as much as the audience. Once, when I was on stage, I caught a glimpse of another comedian staring sadly from the back of the room, red-eyed and full of concern. Another time my act was interrupted by a dead-beat exchange from two artistes at a table beside the stage.

'Is this his act?'

'This is his act.'

Backstage, everyone was excessively polite. 'We're all artistes,' said a pock-faced man in a ginger wig. Other colleagues winked at me, suggested new agents I might contact – 'Don't mention the wife, because she's just died' – recommended other clubs but warned me that such-and-such a place was 'a comic's graveyard'. After my act, I would be told in a friendly but ominous way that I had 'a lot of deaths to die' and even when I seemed to have done well there was always someone who volunteered, 'They were laughing at you, William, not with you.' More general half-truths were often expressed backstage – 'No comedian likes hearing another comedian getting laughs', 'Show business is a very sad profession' and so on. As a beginner, I was also offered bits of practical advice. One night a fat man in Highland dress transferred his wallet to his sporran and told me in his broad accent, 'Always take your money with you on stage, William.'

I worked with ventriloquists, impressionists, magicians, male and female strippers – one lady called herself Jane Eyre – and innumerable drag acts: such was my ignorance of life in general, and sexual matters in particular, that I thought these were real women. Many of my fellow artistes tried to do a bit of everything: comedians would also sing a song, do impressions and even produce a mouth organ or trumpet at the end of their act.

Night after night, I heard the same music: a repertoire of 'Somewhere', 'You're My World', 'Yesterday' and

'Granada' was sometimes enlivened by cha-cha versions of these songs and by other more elaborate and original numbers. I also heard the same jokes, reinforced with swear words, about mothers-in-law, midgets and the fly in the soup.

Some of my fellow performers were shy, lonely figures, who arrived saying, 'I should be out of here by half-past ten' and ended their act with the words, 'Well, that's all from me, folks.'

Others were more flamboyant and genial. 'Thank you, thank you,' I heard these extroverts shouting against their applause. 'And now I'd like to slow down the tempo with that marvellous song . . .' and I heard countless compères giving glowing introductions. 'There's no need to introduce the next act. Films, West End, I think the works . . . Ladies and Gentlemen, put your hands together please for our guest star' – and a bouffant-haired man in a fancy suit would leap confidently to the microphone.

After a few months, I stepped inside a kiosk in the lobby of the big hotel and telephoned the agent with the peculiar voice. This time he sounded not at all pleased to hear from me.

'I'm only booking professional acts,' he said.

'But I am a professional now,' I replied.

'Hold on a moment,' he said unwillingly.

The familiar whispers and titters were followed by the offer of a night's work at the Rising Sun in a suburb called Swinton. I accepted the booking with relief and asked what the fee would be.

'Oh, there's no money in it,' said the agent.

Money was now my biggest problem. The funds I had

saved up had nearly run out and most of my time was now spent on the edge of poverty. Sometimes I ate a bar of slot-machine chocolate instead of a meal and I was extremely grateful when fellow artistes bought me a drink or offered me a cigarette. One day, I was unable to pay for a room at the hostel and spent the night on a bench at the nearby railway station, wrapped in my camel-hair coat but with only one penny in my pocket. The following day I pawned my wrist-watch and fountain pen, telephoned other agents and was met with a chorus of disinterest.

'Leave it to me, my love. Don't concern yourself.' 'Have you fixed Summer Season yet?' 'Lotsa luck. That's the boy' and 'Yes, surely.'

It was now the summer and I learned that various comedians I had worked with were at Llandudno, Lowestoft and other seaside resorts. A singer I had met named Gay Gordon – 'Smashing lady, so down-to-earth' – was now in Majorca.

It was beginning to dawn on me that I had now been black-listed by Manchester's pubs and clubs. Agents still made wild claims – 'I can get you any work you want, except radio and TV' – but nothing materialized. Even unpaid audition appearances were hard to obtain and when I telephoned the man with the funny voice, I heard throat-clearings and muffled words behind a cupped hand, and then was told, 'He's not interested.'

To continue my career I was obliged to seek other audiences. During the summer and autumn of that year, I appeared on stage in Liverpool, Birkenhead, Blackpool and a dozen other places across the Midlands. I usually obtained these bookings on the telephone – I had a plausible telephone manner – and only turned down offers that smacked of amateur theatricals or an amateur night. When I arrived at the club to fulfil my engagement, the management seemed startled. Over and over again, I was told, 'You don't look like a comedian,' and then sometimes, 'Tell us a joke, William.'

Day after day, night after night, I wandered in leaking shoes around heartless centres of these cities – all undergoing the same modernization process – growing increasingly anxious about the performance ahead. Afterwards, I would take the train in pursuit of my next one-night stand. Heaving and weaving on suburban railways through these foreign lands, I would start longing for the familiarity of the city centres. I spent more nights in station waiting-rooms – sometimes heated with a device that required switching on every two minutes and where sleep was therefore impossible. To avoid this particular ordeal I attempted to board night trains.

'Where's this one going to?'

'To Wigan. It's a mail train.'

'Does it stop at Crewe?'

'Yes.'

'Can I get on it?'

'The guards won't let you get on it.'

'I've got to get to Crewe. Does this one go to Crewe?'

'Get in, old man, only we hate people making a habit of it.'

Two hours later, I was told, 'You'd better go and sit down again, old man, because we ain't arrived yet.'

Weeks passed without work. I sat about in the main

hotels of each city before tussling with the lavatory attendant with a clothes brush in hand.

'I'm afraid I can't afford to avail myself of your
services.'

'Have you got threepence for the towel, sir?'

'I'm afraid not.'

The clothes brush would be thrown down angrily and
I would retreat to a cheap café and drink tea from a
saucerless cup. Then I would turn up the collar of my
camel-hair coat, squeeze between the bumpers of parked
cars and strike out along main roads blasted by stinking
buses and lorries.

One dark night, a passer-by shouted, 'Weird bastard!'

The places in which I appeared varied from great barns
with a dozen acts on the bill and perhaps four hundred
people in the audience to little nightclubs with less than a
dozen people present where the compère sometimes rushed
off to fry a steak.

In the larger places, the cabaret was often preceded by
a bingo game – the only thing that kept an audience totally
attentive – and in the smaller places there were fruit
machines and sometimes a miniature casino. In the case of
the latter, the cry of 'Blackjack!' sometimes intruded on
one's performance.

My act became odder, I ceased to tell jokes and started
confronting the audience in a more frantic manner. 'Do you
love me?' I asked. 'Do you fancy me?' In a bid to get some
sort of reaction at last, I jumped into the audience, asked a
woman for a mirror from her bag, quickly stared at my face
in it and started yelping with anguish. In a club where

food was being served, I grabbed chips and other vegetables from people's plates and ate them on stage.

Reactions to these fooleries varied. In a nightclub in Coventry, a patron asked loudly for a pair of ear-plugs, and at a Sunday lunchtime show in Leeds I was hurried down the back stairs by two club officials who feared a disturbance after my performance. Once again the envelope containing my agreed fee had been torn open and half the money in it extracted.

I was not the only comedian to die the death. Many of my fellow artistes had been doing so for years but kept on working thanks to their affable personalities and reliability about turning up on time. Many suffered from ulcers, alcoholism and other troubles of the profession.

At Wolverhampton, a black man stormed off stage, with a gold brassiere in one hand and other items of women's clothing scattered behind him.

'That's the last time I work for Ronnie,' he said, cursing the agent who had booked him.

In Bristol, a singer had claimed that his pocket had been picked while he was on stage. Other acts fumed about their inability to get on to television. 'It's just so ridiculous. Fred always does a bomb,' complained the wife of one comic who was something of a star on the club circuit but had never been invited inside a television studio.

This particular man had actually taken me under his wing, driving me one night from Stoke-on-Trent to Derby in a silencer-broken Austin A40, announcing as he did so, 'This is the cradle of so-called tradition comedy.'

I had seen placards outside clubs announcing Fred as

an 'outstanding attraction' and had seen him on stage, pulverizing the audience, taking his applause and then joining me at my table and hurling a cigarette at me in a careless gesture of triumph.

I had asked Fred if he had ever appeared at The Man In The Moon and he said, 'Many times.' I asked him what he thought of the agent with the girlish voice. 'I thought him just pathetic. I nearly broke his neck.'

Sometimes I shared the same lodgings as these people and began to keep theatrical hours.

'Have you eaten?' asked Fred at five o'clock one afternoon.

Usually, I preferred more anonymous accommodation, mixing with travelling salesmen in the cheaper hotels. Whenever I could afford it, I would try to restore my confidence by travelling First Class, staying in the best hotel in the town and choosing dishes on the menu accompanied by items such as 'button mushrooms' and 'a Madeira sauce'. Thanks to these particular indulgences, poverty was always close at hand and at one low point I found myself enquiring about where I might pawn my clothes. Once, I left my suitcase at a left-luggage office in Leeds and was unable to retrieve it for several days. I was obliged to wear the same shirt every day and eventually appeared on stage not having brushed my teeth since the previous weekend. Without the regular application of sun-tan lotion, my face had a deathly pallor under the lights, and fellow artistes were moved to wonder about my health.

'You don't look too well, William.'

After thirteen months on the boards, my theatrical fever had to some extent abated. The anxiety I experienced at each appearance – the shaking and sweating – was much greater than when I had begun. The crazy confidence and egotism of youth had dwindled away. I was now twenty years old and had begun to come to my senses, though no alternative occupation had occurred to me and I faced the future with fear.

As my theatrical career drew to a close, my engagements became more and more far-flung. My last appearance as a professional comedian took place in a tiny Welsh mining village halfway up the Merthyr Vale. I took a bus up the valley in gathering darkness. Slag heaps higher than real hills loomed to left and right. Smoke poured from the chimneys of terraced houses. When I reached the village, I heard the din of electronic music and found the working men's club already packed. The audience was out of control by the time I stepped on to the large empty stage. As I skipped and danced towards the microphone, an old woman imitated the sound of a sheep.

In the chaos that followed, I shouted and screamed for attention.